Nevermore

Nevermore

Linda Newbery

Illustrated by
Ian P. Benfold Haywood

Orion
Children's Books

First published in Great Britain in 2008
by Orion Children's Books
a division of the Orion Publishing Group Ltd
Orion House
5 Upper St Martin's Lane
London WC2H 9EA
An Hachette Livre UK Company

1 3 5 7 9 10 8 6 4 2

A catalogue record for this book is available
from the British Library.

ISBN 978 1 84255 547 7

Printed in Great Britain by Clays Ltd, St Ives plc

The Orion Publishing Group's policy is to use papers
that are natural, renewable and recyclable products made from
wood grown in sustainable forests. The logging and manufacturing
processes are expected to conform to the environmental
regulations of the country of origin.

www.orionbooks.co.uk

For Pakie, Fionnuala and Jean O'Callaghan –
Le gach dea ghui

Contents

1
The House on the Hillside

'We might as well *live* in this van,' Tizzie complained. 'We spend our whole life in it.'

'Oh, do cheer up.' Tizzie's mum didn't sound too cheerful herself. 'I told you, it'll be different this time.' She leaned forward, peering at the lane ahead through the *wish, wish* of windscreen wipers.

'It won't be different.' Tizzie was slumped in the passenger seat, clutching her new furry pencil-case. 'It'll be the same as always. I'll just start to get used to it, then you'll want to move again.' Shrugged into moodiness, she wore it like a coat, even though part of her wanted to wriggle out of it and stamp it to the floor.

1

Mum halted at a crossroads, and frowned at the signpost, an old-fashioned one with white arms pointing in four directions.

'Why does it have to rain?' Tizzie grumbled.

'Because it does. It might stop soon.'

'I suppose we're lost now,' said Tizzie, wiping the side window with her sleeve. There was nothing in any direction but rainswept fields and hedges. They were on high level ground, though she'd lost all sense of direction since they'd left the motorway. 'I thought you knew the way?'

'I do, but it looks different in the mist. Sleet. That's what I'm looking for. Why doesn't it say Sleet?'

'What, Sleet's the name of a *place*?'

'The nearest village to where we're going.'

Mum edged the van forward and turned right into a lane which soon plunged downhill between high walls; and now here was a village. Stone houses and cottages were pressed tightly together on both sides of the narrow street. No one was around. It looked as wet and dismal as everywhere else they'd passed through. There wasn't even a pavement, and water flowed in a dark torrent down both sides of the road.

'Oh! We're here. This *is* Sleet,' said Mum. Ahead, at a T-junction, was a small shop, with the name *Sleet Village Store* above the window, and a red Post Office sign. *Closed,* said the sign on the door.

A Post-It note with directions written on it was stuck to the dashboard, but Mum didn't glance at it as she slowed for the junction, then turned left by a church. 'Got it now,' she muttered.

'Hey, this looks exciting.' Tizzie looked out at wet stone and dripping foliage. 'It's really great we've come to live in a place called Sleet, in the middle of nowhere. With one manky shop that's not even open.'

'Stop it, Tizzie! You're not helping. You'll see Roven Mere in a minute.'

'Can't wait,' said Tizzie, in the flat, dull voice that seemed to speak *for* her. Once it started, she couldn't shut it up. And, really, she *was* curious about Roven Mere. The name. The way her Mum had described it.

'You'll like it,' Mum had told her, after announcing that they'd be moving yet again. 'It's like nowhere else. Huge. Old. And right out in the country.'

Tizzie didn't know Country. She was used to London. She knew Hoxton and Eltham and Penge, Catford and Brent and Tooting, the bits they'd lived in. Before those, before she could remember, there had been others. Flats, streets, shops, were what she knew, and sometimes a park, and the cafés and small restaurants her mum had worked in. There had been schools, too many different ones to count: the play-grounds and the classrooms and the teachers whose names she could never remember. And all the faces: friendly or hostile, curious or uninterested.

There'd be no getting away from that, just because this was Country. She'd catch the bus to school with other children from the village, Mum had told her; she'd soon make friends. 'What's the point?' Tizzie retorted. 'Every time I get a friend, you decide we're moving again. You do it on purpose.'

This time, it was Kamila she was leaving behind. Kamila had promised to text every day, and had given her the tiger pencil-case as a leaving present. But texting wouldn't be the same as having someone to be with, someone to talk and giggle with.

'It'll be different this time,' Mum had promised.

Tizzie didn't know why she kept saying that. Why *should* it be different? Mum never stayed anywhere for long.

'Here,' Mum said now, slowing for a bend. 'See, down there.'

Below them, a valley opened out. Rain-lashed fields and woods dropped down to a stream, climbing steeply again on the far side. She could see only one house: a many-chimneyed stone mansion tucked against the hillside, roofed in slate that gleamed purple-grey in the wet. A single turret rose against the backdrop of trees.

'What – you mean that's it?'

Mum nodded. 'That's where we're going. That's Roven Mere.' She pressed her lips together in a tight, determined smile. Expert at reading her mother's moods, Tizzie knew that this putting-the-best-face-on-it could easily shatter into bad temper and shouting. Perhaps Mum already knew she'd made a mistake.

'What does it mean?' Tizzie asked. 'Roven Mere?'

Mum shrugged. 'Mere? It's a kind of lake, isn't it? I told you there's a lake.'

'And Roven? What's that? *Raven* Mere would make more sense.'

'How should I know?' Mum threw her a glance. 'Maybe someone just made it up. Liked the sound of it.'

So Tizzie said no more as her mother steered the van round a bend, the house now disappearing from view behind woodland. Beyond the trees, Mum pulled up at a big entrance with gates of black wrought-iron. A signboard said ROVEN MERE. PRIVATE PROPERTY. STRICTLY NO ENTRANCE WITHOUT PERMISSION. A small house, built of stone with a wooden porch, stood alongside.

'That's just the lodge,' said Mum. 'Get out and open the gates! Don't just sit there.'

'But it says "No Entrance",' Tizzie pointed out.

'Don't be silly. They're expecting us.'

'So why didn't they leave the gates open?'

Mum's eyes rolled. 'Just do it, will you?'

Tizzie unfastened her seat-belt, pushed back the door and slid down. She'd forgotten about the furry tiger pencil-case on her lap; it flumped to the ground. Cold rain beat into her face and ears as she bent to pick it up; luckily it had fallen on wet gravel, not into a muddy puddle. She stroked the tiger's damp fur as she replaced it on her seat. Mum saw, of course, and said, 'You'll ruin that if you keep throwing it about. You ought to look after your things.'

'What do *you* care?' Tizzie shouted. 'What do you care about anything?' Her eyes blurred as she turned to the gates; she had to blink away angry tears before she could see what to do. There was a heavy latch to slide back, then she had to push the gates open one at a time. The hinges made a grating screech; then the van's tyres crunched on gravel as Mum drove through and waited for her to close the gates behind.

Tizzie would rather have walked, getting soaked through to make her point, but she got back in, dripping. She didn't complain, but just as if she had, Mum said, 'We'll get wetter than that, unloading.'

The driveway turned sharp right along the hillside, below the line of trees that now reared above. Tizzie felt herself shrinking in the passenger seat as the house, tall and forbidding with many shuttered windows, loomed ahead. It had a grand entrance, with pillars on each side, and a big wooden door that looked very firmly shut.

I can't live in a place like this — I just can't! she thought. *I don't know how to!*

2
The Puddled Courtyard

'Finnigan,' said Mum. 'That's who we've got to find. We can't get in till we find him.'

Tizzie pulled up her hood. 'Who's Finnigan?'

'He's in charge here,' said Mum, jangling the van keys in her hand. 'I told you.'

Tizzie was quite sure Mum *hadn't* told her, but didn't say so. They were standing in a puddled courtyard, with stables on two sides, garages on another, and two archways: one leading in, the other out, continuing the driveway they'd come in on.

'*Mr* Finnigan?' Tizzie asked. 'Or is he Lord Finnigan, or something like that? Does he own this place, then?'

She felt silly, not knowing these things. They'd had plenty of time on the journey from London; why hadn't Mum told her? But Mum was never very talkative, and didn't like being questioned. 'Oh, don't go *on,* Tizzie!' she'd say, with an irritable swish of her pony-tail. Tizzie had learned that there were sometimes other ways of finding out what she wanted to know. And sometimes there weren't.

'Finnigan, that's all,' Mum answered, not really listening. She was looking back along the driveway, and Tizzie saw that someone was coming. Or, rather, a large black umbrella was advancing towards them, its spike tilted forward like a weapon. All Tizzie could see was the bottom half of a pink raincoat, and a pair of feet. This couldn't be Finnigan, as the hem of a skirt was visible below the raincoat, as well as plump pale ankles. The feet, in stout lace-up shoes, walked briskly, swerving around the puddles.

The umbrella marched all the way to the van before swinging upright to reveal a square, reddish face, with small eyes and a straight mouth. On top, grey hair sprang up and back, lacquered into stiff waves like a hair-helmet.

'You can't park here,' said the mouth. 'It's private property. The house isn't open to visitors.'

'Who are you?' Mum said rudely. 'I'm looking for Finnigan.'

'And you are?'

'Morag Furlong.' Mum spoke in the *what's-it-to-you?* way that Tizzie sometimes got told off for when she tried it at school.

'Oh yes, our new cook.' The small eyes fixed on Tizzie. 'And you are—?'

'Tizzie,' said Tizzie. 'Tizzie Furlong.'

Rather alarmingly, the mouth spread itself into a smile, showing big square teeth. 'Oh, I like that. Tizzie! I used to have an old Aunt Tizzie.' The eyes softened. 'Short for Thirza, that was. You're welcome here, lovey, very very welcome. Both of you.'

Lovey! Tizzie stifled a giggle.

'It's short for Elizabeth,' said Mum shortly. 'Not Thirza.'

'Well, I'm pleased to meet you both. I hope you'll be happy here.' A hand thrust itself at Tizzie, and she realised she was expected to shake it; then the gesture was repeated with Mum.

Tizzie knew, though this woman couldn't be expected to know, how Mum disliked touching people. Instead of doing proper shaking, Mum made the briefest possible contact with the soft ringed hand before dropping it; then she wiped her own hand several times on her wet jeans.

'I'm Mrs Crump,' said the older woman. 'Elsa, but Finnigan calls me Mrs Crump. You'll be meeting my son and grandson.'

Mum looked bored. 'Where *is* Finnigan?'

'He's usually busy, this time of day. Best get yourselves settled in. You're in Cloud Cottage, next to the orchard.'

'I know,' said Mum. 'Finnigan told me when he gave me the job.'

Tizzie huffed, but no one noticed. Why hadn't Mum *said*? Tizzie had imagined them living in that vast mansion, somewhere along a dark corridor. Instead, Cloud Cottage! She liked the name. She imagined it as a tree-house, balanced in swaying branches, up in the rain.

'Down through the arch,' Mrs Crump went on. 'You can't miss it. You've got your own parking place down there. Key's in the door and everything ready for you. Come over to the house when you've moved your bags in. I'll have tea made.'

Tea! Tizzie pictured a large table spread with sandwiches and cake. Her stomach was hollow; it seemed an age since they'd eaten the plastic-wrapped sandwiches bought from a service station.

'Then you can get settled into your kitchen,' Mrs Crump added to Mum.

It was funny about Mum and food. She never bothered much about food for herself and Tizzie, but she loved cooking. She loved cooking as she loved nothing else, it seemed to Tizzie. Cooking was her job, so at least she was happy when she was working. She cooked like an angel, everyone said. Which was a strange thing to say, Tizzie always thought – did angels *do* cooking? You never saw them eating, so why would they? Besides, anyone less like an angel than Mum she could hardly imagine. Angels, in Tizzie's experience, were pale gauzy creatures on top of Christmas trees, or translucent in stained glass; Mum was fierce and scowly. Not much like a mum, either. Not like other people's mums.

'Don't stand there daydreaming!' she was saying. 'Get back in.'

And, turning her back on Mrs Crump, she climbed into the driver's seat, while Tizzie went round to the passenger side. Mum hadn't put on her coat; her jeans and striped sweatshirt were dark with rain, her hair lank and wet in its pony-tail. She rarely worried about things like mere comfort. Tizzie, shivering inside her jacket, was colder than she'd have thought possible at the beginning of June. Was this what it was like, out in the country? But she felt cheered by the prospect of tea and a welcome. And Mrs Crump had a son and a grandson, so there were other people here. Well, of course there were – Mum was going to cook for them. Tizzie tried to imagine who might live in a place like this. What did they *do* all day?

'Where's this orchard then?' Mum said, turning on the ignition.

Tizzie pointed through the archway to a field of low trees. 'Don't you know the way? I thought you told Mrs Crump you've seen the cottage.'

'No,' said Mum, looking round as she backed the van. 'Finnigan offered to take me down there, but I was in a hurry.'

Too much of a hurry to see where you're going to live? Tizzie nearly retorted, but said instead, 'She was nice, wasn't she? Mrs Crump?'

Mum only grunted in reply. She drove slowly along the track – a muddy, puddly one, not gravelled like the main driveway – towards a small white cottage that stood on its own behind a paling fence. 'Now Tizz, you're not to go making yourself a nuisance. I know what you're like.'

But, Tizzie thought as Mum pulled up alongside the fence, *do* you? Do you really know what I'm like? Or do you only know what you *think* I'm like?

An odder thought struck her. Do *I* really know what I'm like? Is this just the Me that other people think they know – the Me that other people have made? And how can I tell which bits of me are the *real* Me?

'Any chance of a hand with these bags?' Mum was already round at the back. 'Or do I have to do everything myself?'

3

The Window-Seat

C loud Cottage had oddly-shaped rooms and twisty stairs. It had a fireplace and flowered curtains, and small windows with diamond-shaped panes. It had a blue-painted front door with a horse-shoe knocker. It made Tizzie think of the gingerbread house in Hansel and Gretel – except that no witch lived in this cottage, nor, apparently, anyone else.

Tizzie put down her bag at the bottom of the stairs. 'What, is all this for us? Or are we sharing with someone?'

'No, just us. It's a bit twee, but it'll do.'

'A whole house!' Stretching out both arms, Tizzie

twirled round in the unaccustomed space. 'A whole little house, all to ourselves! Luxury!'

'I wouldn't get too excited. It's nothing special.'

'It *is* special!' Tizzie retorted, eager to explore.

The ground floor consisted of the sitting-room with its cushiony sofa and chair facing the fireplace, and a tiny kitchen behind. Mum sniffed at that, then led the way up to the first floor. Here there was one bedroom, next to the bathroom, and another up its own flight of stairs. Tizzie ran up to look. Immediately she wanted this attic room for herself.

'You can have it,' said Mum. 'I'm not running up and down two lots of stairs.'

'A room each!' Tizzie was amazed; she and Mum usually had to share, or, once or twice when she *did* have a room to herself, it had been half-full of junk. But this! She loved it – roof-shaped, up in the eaves. A small window, with a cushioned seat for a window-sill, looked over the orchard, where stumpy trees stood in lines, holding out their branches to the rain. Everything was hazed in soft green, the distances blurred into mist. Tizzie ran over to perch sideways on the window-seat, her nose to the cold, rain-streaked glass. 'I wonder who gave the cottage its name? It feels like sitting in a cloud,' she remarked. But Mum's feet were already clumping back down the stairs; she hadn't heard.

Tizzie got up and had a good look round her room. The bed had iron railings at head and foot, and someone had made it up, with plumped pillows and a

14

dark-red bedspread. There was a tall wooden wardrobe and a chest-of-drawers with two shelves above; no other furniture, and the floor was bare boards, with a rug by the bed made from tatters of fabric. No posters or pictures anywhere, and certainly no TV or radio.

Hearing Mum moving around the room below, unpacking, Tizzie ran down for her own bag, and brought it up. It didn't take long to find places for her few clothes and belongings. Then she reached into her rucksack, pulled out her mobile phone, and sat on the bed to text Kamila. She'd promised to send a text as soon as she arrived.

No signal.

What? She couldn't send text messages? How was she meant to sur*vive*? She sat aghast, gazing at the roof-slopes of her room, the cracked white plaster and the uneven stairs leading down. The realisation surged into her that she was stranded here, miles from anywhere, miles from everyone she knew, with no way of communicating.

No other house could be seen from the window; just the orchard, a high hedge, and fields beyond.

This place might be all right for a holiday, but how was she going to live here? What would she do? Where would she go? Where were the shops, the cinema, the High Street? She'd be *stranded* here, away from everything she knew.

'Mum!' she yelled down.

'What?'

Tizzie stomped down. 'I can't get a signal for my mobile!'

Mum was hanging clothes in her wardrobe. 'No, I don't suppose you can. We're in a valley here.'

'Why didn't you *tell* me? How am I meant to phone Kamila?'

'There's a phone downstairs. You can use that now and then, only don't run up a huge bill.'

'But it's not the same!' Tizzie grumped.

'No, it's not the same. Things are different from now on. You'd better start getting used to it.'

'But – why different? How different?' Tizzie didn't understand.

'It's just the way it is.' Mum took a bundle of socks from her bag, and stuffed them in a drawer. Then she shoved the empty bag in the bottom of her wardrobe. 'There, that's done. I'm going up to the house now. You'd better come too.'

Tizzie looked at her, recognising her *don't-pester-me* expression. They went down to the van. There were two boxes still in the back. One was for the cottage – CDs, a few books, a fan heater. The other, bigger and heavier, was full of Mum's cooking equipment: her chopping and carving knives, her graters, reamers, measuring spoons, scoops and sieves, scales and whisks and ladles, and – most important of all – her folders of recipes. Mum shouldered this box, first

16

handing Tizzie two saucepans and a wok to make it less top-heavy.

'Won't they have their own kitchen stuff here?' Tizzie asked.

'I like to know I've got everything I need.'

It was still raining hard, so Tizzie put the wok on her head like a helmet. Mum marched ahead, shoes squelching, her blonde pony-tail dripping down her back.

'Oh, for Pete's sake!' she said, turning round, and seeing Tizzie wearing the wok. 'They'll think you're five years old!'

'Who's Pete?' Tizzie said, just to annoy. How unfair Mum was! The wok was a perfectly effective rain-hat.

Mum said no more as they walked through the courtyard and up the drive towards the mansion. Tizzie wondered again why she kept insisting that things were different now. *What* was different, exactly? They'd never been in a place like this before – but there was nothing very different about moving. Tizzie had lived in so many flats above cafés, so many dingy rooms and bedsits, that she couldn't even remember them all.

'That must be so cool!' Kamila had said, once. 'Like you're a gipsy in a painted caravan, always going somewhere new.'

'*You* try it, then,' Tizzie had told her. 'See how you like it.'

They'd been sitting in Kamila's bedroom – her luxurious bedroom, big enough to invite friends into,

17

with its sofa and TV and shelves full of books, and pictures from magazines pinned to a board. Kamila had a wardrobe full of clothes: a whole rail of them, all hers. Skirts and tops and trousers and coats; saris and shalwar kameez in gorgeous glowing colours, presents from her aunties.

Sometimes, after school, they tried on clothes, posing and preening in front of the full-length mirror on the wardrobe door. In turquoise silk trousers, beaded sandals, and a matching tunic jewelled in deep red, Tizzie stared at herself in the mirror and pretended she was someone else entirely. Kamila braided Tizzie's hair back, gave her wristfuls of bangles to wear and made up her eyes with kohl, and then she really *did* look different from her usual self. Mysterious. A girl of secrets. Only her hair spoiled the overall look: it wasn't dark enough, too gingery, too rusty.

'You look great!' Kamila told her. 'I'd give you the shalwar kameez, only my Auntie Shaheen wouldn't like it.'

Kamila had so much. She had a little brother and an older sister. She had a dad as well as a mum. She had aunties and uncles and cousins and second cousins who were always coming to visit at weekends, for delicious meals that went on all afternoon. Her house was usually full of laughter and the smell of spicy cooking.

Sometimes, Tizzie wondered why she'd missed out on all this. She had no dad, no grandad, no aunts or uncles. There was just her and Mum, and Nannina, who lived on her own in a flat in Battersea. No more family than that.

And now she was miles from her only friend, as well.

4

The Cavernous Kitchen

Instead of going in at the grand front door they'd seen as they approached in the van, Mum turned left, heading for the side of the house. Tizzie saw a flagged terrace with a walled garden below; and, through an arch, a brick path, the dazzling green of a lawn, and a mass of sodden foliage. From this side, facing the valley, the house looked less stern, though it reared above her to at least three storeys. Tall windows overlooked the garden; behind railings, stone steps led down to a door.

'Down here.' Mum had tucked the file of recipes under her sweatshirt to keep it dry, giving her a peculiar boxy shape, while the cardboard box she carried on her shoulder was sagging soggily. 'You'll have to get the door,' she told Tizzie. 'I haven't got a spare hand.'

Tizzie turned the handle and pushed firmly. Inside was a vast kitchen, the biggest she'd ever seen, with a wooden table stretching almost the whole length. One end was taken up by a brick fireplace, where a log burned in the grate. A log fire, in June! But Tizzie was so cold and wet that the warmth drew her in.

The bulky shape of Mrs Crump rose from a seat by the fire. 'Oh, look at you! Pair of drowned rats!' She took the soggy box from Mum, the saucepans and wok from Tizzie, and ushered both of them towards the fireplace. 'Come on in. Get yourselves warm.'

Tizzie could think of nothing nicer than to sit in the warming glow of the fire. She shuffled forward, dripping.

'Bring another chair up, lovey!' Mrs Crump called over her shoulder, and Tizzie saw that there was someone else in the kitchen – a boy of about her own age, with thick brown hair like a thatched roof. He wore a maroon sweatshirt with an emblem on it, a white shirt-collar showing underneath. He was sitting at the farthest end of the table, eating sultanas from a packet.

'My grandson, Davy,' Mrs Crump explained. 'He's always ravenous when he gets in from school. Davy, this is Mrs Furlong, our new cook, and Tizzie.'

Mum glared. 'Not Mrs. I'm not married. Morag will do fine.'

'Oh. Sorry,' said Mrs Crump, looking a bit startled.

The boy lugged a wooden chair over to the fireplace, and said, 'Hi,' looking at Tizzie. He had a wide, friendly smile, and dark brown eyes.

'Hello,' Tizzie said back, feeling shy and awkward.

'I expect you two'll soon be friends,' Mrs Crump said comfortably. 'It'll be nice to have a friend your own age living here, won't it, Davy? I'll just top up the pot, and we'll have tea.'

Tizzie glanced at Davy again, then away, quickly. She wasn't sure how good she was at making friends. Certainly she wasn't very good at *keeping* them. How could she be?

'You'll be going to school with Davy next week,' Mrs Crump told her. 'He's in year seven, same as you.'

Tizzie shrugged. It made little difference to her which school she went to. She wanted to be friendlier, but was very conscious of both Mum and Mrs Crump watching. It made her feel big and clumsy, unable to put words together in the way she wanted. But Mrs Crump obviously expected her to be interested, so she managed, 'How do we get there?'

'Bus. Stops outside the Black Lion, twenty-past eight. You can go together – that'll be nice.' Mrs Crump opened a door in the corner, and walked into a larder that looked quite big enough to be a room in itself. Tizzie saw shelves and shelves stacked with cans and packets, bottles and jars.

There was a silence. The log in the grate sank lower, with a comfortable settling sound, releasing a scent of ashy wood-smoke. Someone ought to say something, Tizzie thought, but couldn't think of anything. Davy didn't seem to mind; he was pulling at a loose thread on the sleeve of his sweatshirt.

After a few moments, Mrs Crump emerged from the larder, carrying a large covered plate. Putting it on the table, she lifted the domed lid with a *ta-dah!* flourish to reveal a sponge cake layered with jam and sprinkled with icing sugar. 'I made this yesterday. It's not as good as you can do, I'm sure,' she told Mum, 'being a trained cook and all, but I did get second prize at the village show with one like it.'

'It looks very nice,' Tizzie said politely, since Mum made no response. What was the matter with her? She'd gone even more gruff and silent than usual. Perhaps this cavernous, old-fashioned kitchen had put her off – it was so different from the last one she'd worked in, at Mr Lo's Wing Wah restaurant in Tooting, all stainless steel and streamlined. Still, Mum must have seen this when she came for the interview. It couldn't be a surprise to her.

Even Mrs Crump, tirelessly cheerful, must have noticed. 'Can you pour the tea, Tizzie love, and I'll cut the cake?'

A tray was ready with cups and saucers, milk jug, and sugar cubes in a bowl with silver tongs.

Tizzie did so. 'Is everyone having tea?'

'Squash for Davy, dear. He doesn't like tea. He can get it himself.'

Although Tizzie would have preferred squash, she

resigned herself to tea. Mrs Crump handed round slices of cake on flowered plates.

'How many people live here?' Tizzie asked. With such an enormous kitchen as this – and she could see another room beyond, with sinks and cupboards and shelves – she felt sure there must be dozens.

'Well, let's see.' Mrs Crump had moved a chair closer to the fire; Davy perched on a stool. 'There's me and Davy, and Davy's dad—'

'He's the gardener,' Davy said, his mouth full of cake.

'We're at Mere Lodge, by the main gates. Then there's old Jack Doughty – he's been here longer than anyone else. He's got a flat above the stables. Finnigan, of course – he's in charge of everything. Apart from that, it's the girls that do the cleaning and laundry – girls, I call them! They're grown women. They come in from the village every day. I think that's it.'

'Yes,' said Tizzie. 'But all those people – they're like, well, servants. I meant who *lives* here – in this house?'

'Oh.' Mrs Crump looked at her curiously. 'It belongs to Lord Rupert. Lord Rupert Evershall. Surely your mum must have told you that?'

Mum gave a little huffing laugh, that could have meant anything; hotness prickled over Tizzie's face. 'I expect she did,' she lied, 'and I just forgot.' She darted an accusing look at Mum, who wouldn't meet her eye. How infuriating it was, having to make herself look dim-witted and slow, rather than admit that her mother never told her anything!

'Well, there's a lot for you to take in, coming to a

big old place like this,' said Mrs Crump.

Mum had taken no more than two bites of cake, then put the plate down in the hearth as if it might do for some passing dog. Mrs Crump noticed; Tizzie saw her look of tight-lipped disappointment. But she didn't remark on it, instead turning to Tizzie. 'Another piece of sponge, dear? You must be famished after your journey.'

'Yes, please.' Tizzie didn't really want it, but felt that she had to make up for Mum's off-handedness. *I* can be polite and friendly, even if *she* can't, she told herself.

She wondered what a Lord might look like. Into her mind floated a picture of a tall and rather stern man, wearing a scarlet robe trimmed with fur. He wore knee-breeches and white stockings, and shoes with big buckles. What should he have on his head? Not a crown, but surely a Lord would wear some kind of headgear, to show that he wasn't just an ordinary person. How amazing to think that she might meet someone so important – a real Lord! She might bump into him in the courtyard or the garden! Would she have to curtsey? Call him *your Lordship*? Or would it be better to run away and hide?

'Is he very grand, Lord Rupert?' she asked.

'Oh, I've never actually met him,' said Mrs Crump. 'None of us has. Only Finnigan. We're expecting him home in a week or two. Him and the family. Very exciting it'll be, meeting them at last!'

Tizzie glanced at Mum, who was leafing through

her folder of recipes as if this had nothing to do with her.

'Is he married? Is there a *Lady* Someone?' Tizzie asked. She thought she could get away with one more question before Mum told her to be quiet and stop making a nuisance of herself.

'Yes, dear. And a daughter, same age as you and Davy. Twelve, she is.'

'Oh! Will she—'

'Tizzie!' Mum gave her a sharp look. 'I've got work to do, and I'm sure Mrs Crump has too. You'd better go back to the cottage, or explore outside.'

Mrs Crump began stacking the tea things on the tray. 'Davy can show you round, can't you, Davy? You must be wondering what sort of a place you've come to live in,' she added to Tizzie.

Tizzie glanced at Davy, expecting him to pull a *do I have to?* face, but instead he said, 'OK,' dabbed up the last cake-crumbs from his plate, and stood up. 'Come on. We'll go this way.'

He went through a door on the opposite side of the kitchen from the one Tizzie and her mother had entered by. Going after him, Tizzie heard Mrs Crump saying to Mum, 'Poor little lamb! She must be quite bewildered, bless her!' and Mum's reply, 'Oh, Tizzie can cope. She's used to changes. She's really very sensible.' Tizzie wasn't entirely sure that *very sensible* was how she wanted to be described; and how surprising that Mum thought of her that way! Mum never said anything like that to her face.

She had followed Davy into a long corridor that

ran the length of the house, with doors on both sides, and cupboards and shelves at intervals. As it was below ground-level, it was cool and only dimly-lit.

'This is the office – Finnigan works in there sometimes,' Davy told her, as they passed an open door; Tizzie glimpsed cabinets and two desks, shelves of files, and a computer-screen. 'Most of these other rooms aren't used any more, except things are kept in some of them. In the old days they'd have been store-rooms and cellars. One was just for boots and shoes, and one was a gun-room.'

'Is it really old, the house?'

Davy turned left to a flight of stairs leading up. 'Some of it's as old as Queen Elizabeth the First. But lots of bits and pieces have been added on since. There's stairs and attics and little doors all over the place, and more rooms than I've even counted. Here. This is the ground floor.'

He opened a door and went through, Tizzie following. As it swung shut behind them, she saw that it fitted into the wood panelling so closely that it was hard to see a door at all.

5

The Puppet Room

They had emerged into a sort of room-between-rooms, wood-panelled, bare apart from one upright chair, an Indian rug, and a vase of lilies on a table. 'This way's the dining-room,' Davy said, opening one of two larger and more obvious doors.

The dining-room was long and low, gallery-shaped, with windows looking out to the terrace and the gardens below. It was dominated by a long table, as big as the one in the kitchen – but this one was made of conker-coloured wood, and polished to a mirror-like sheen. Although the table was extensive enough to seat twenty or more diners, only three places were set: one at the head of the table, with a big carver chair, and one to each side of that. The remainder of the table stretched, empty and shining, almost the length of the room.

Tizzie moved closer to look. Each place-setting had an array of silver cutlery, two crystal goblets, and a ruby-red napkin embellished with the letter 'E'. It looked as if someone was expected to dinner; but she'd just come up from the kitchen, and no meal was being cooked there. The chairs were high-backed and of the same dark wood, with the letter 'E' embroidered on the tapestry seats.

'E for − what was that name?' Tizzie wondered aloud. 'Ever-something?'

'Evershall,' Davy said. 'Like *ever shall be, the power and the glory, for ever and ever, Amen.*'

His words sounded too loud in the quiet room. The air was hushed and silent, as if no one had disturbed it recently.

'What's all this ready for?' Tizzie asked him. 'Is someone coming?'

'No,' he answered. 'It's always like this. No one ever comes.'

'It feels like the house is waiting.'

'That's because it is.' Davy ran his finger along the carved top of a chair-back. 'Always waiting.'

'But your gran said they'd be coming home in a week or two! Lord Evershall and the family?'

Davy shrugged. 'You'll get used to that. It's what they're always saying. Always coming soon. Always in a week or two. It never gets any nearer. You'll see.'

'But everything's ready – flowers, and everything!' She gestured towards a bowl of lilies in the centre of the table. Their heady scent, almost sickeningly sweet, filled her senses.

'My gran does the flowers,' said Davy. 'That's one of her jobs.'

'But what's the point of doing flowers, if no one's coming?'

Tizzie's head was thrumming with questions. How long had Lord Rupert been gone, if Mrs Crump had never even met him? Why would someone own a huge house like this, and keep staff to run it, but then not live here?

Davy was moving away, towards the far end of the room. 'See here?' He looked round to see if she was following, then opened another concealed door in the panelling, at waist height.

Expecting just a cupboard stacked with plates and dishes, Tizzie looked in and was surprised to find herself looking down a dark drop, like a lift shaft. Voices wafted up, and she looked at Davy in startlement as she recognised her mother's crisp tones: 'I want Post-It notes on all these cupboards till I've learned what's what.'

Davy was grinning at her surprise. 'That's the kitchen, underneath. This thing's called a dumb waiter. See these cords? See that platform down there? They put the plates on that, and the waiter up here pulls the cords, and the food comes up. Otherwise it'd mean loads of traipsing up the stairs, and the food would be cold by the time it got here. The dirty dishes go down that way, too.'

'That's clever!'

'I think lots of old houses have them. Come on, let's go upstairs. These downstairs rooms are mainly boring, just chairs and tables and vases and stuff. Upstairs is better.'

They went back the way they'd come, through into a room with three sofas arranged round a fireplace, and into a square entrance-hall. From the windows, Tizzie saw the rain-swept driveway and tousled trees, and the pillared porch she'd seen from the van on the way in. Umbrellas were propped in a stand by the front door, and today's *Times* was neatly folded on a table. An archway led through to a broad staircase with a banister that swept down, ending in a flourishing twirl.

Davy bounded up the stairs, two at a time.

'Are we allowed?' Tizzie called after him.

'Course! Finnigan doesn't mind, long as we don't break anything. There's no one else.'

Half-way up, the stairs reached a landing with a big window, then doubled back on themselves, rising to the next floor. Not stopping, Davy went on to the second storey, and continued along a corridor. The ceiling here was lower, the doors and wood-panelling much plainer. Tizzie had the idea that she was still at the front of the house, the side that faced the driveway.

'These rooms are like a museum,' Davy told her. 'That's what I call it, anyway.'

He opened the first door on the left. Looking in, Tizzie saw more paintings than she'd ever seen in one room, covering every wall, reaching right up to the ceiling: portraits and landscapes and miniatures, and some that looked like children's paintings.

'Whose are they?'

'Finnigan's,' said Davy.

'What, you mean he painted all these?'

'No,' Davy said. 'He collects them, and cleans them, and frames them.' He closed the door, and moved on to the next. This time Tizzie was confronted by rows of masks: masks made of feathers or jewels, or in the shape of wolves' faces or owl heads. She felt a tingle down her back: there was something creepy about all those blank eye-shapes, and their empty stares.

'Did Finnigan make these, too?' she asked.

'He makes all sorts of things,' Davy said. 'You'll see.'

The room he showed her next was full of wood-carvings – clocks, toys, animals – on shelves or in cases, or mounted on the walls. Tizzie would have liked to spend more time looking and wondering, but Davy moved on to the next room.

Opening the door, he flicked a light-switch inside. Tizzie blinked, dazzled by spotlights on a track on the ceiling. Blinds concealed the windows, so that the room was lit dramatically.

'Look behind you!' Davy said.

Tizzie turned, and gave an exclamation of surprise. Most of one wall was taken up by an old-fashioned puppet theatre, curtained in deep blue, with the 'E' emblem in gold thread on the canopy. A painted backdrop showed a seaside promenade, with sparkling waves fading to the horizon. Two stringed puppets hung behind the canopy: a fat pink lady in a ruffled bathing costume that covered her from neck to ankles, and a boy in a sailor-suit. Their hands and feet were limp at the ends of their strings, and their heads drooped.

'A real puppet theatre!' Tizzie had only seen them in story-books. 'Whose is it?'

'Finnigan made it,' said Davy. 'He's clever like that.' He reached in and plucked a string. The boy's arm, ingeniously jointed, made an oddly human movement, as if wanting to shake hands.

The Finnigan who made and looked after all these things was beginning to seem very different from the one Tizzie had imagined. Before this, she'd pictured him stern and strict in a business suit, sitting in his office, adding up accounts on a computer, giving orders to the staff, and checking up on them. But the Finnigan who made toys and masks couldn't be anything like that.

'What's it all for?' she asked.

'For?'

'I mean, who does puppet shows here? Who sees them? It ought to be in a fairground, or at the seaside, where children can come and watch. Does it go to places like that, with someone to work the puppets?'

Davy shook his head. 'It just stays here. It's Greta's.'

'Greta's?'

'Greta Evershall. Lord Rupert's daughter. This is all for her.'

'But why?'

Davy shrugged. 'Just the way it is.'

Tizzie said eagerly, 'Have you met her?'

'No! I've never met any of them. No one has, only Finnigan. He's been here longer than anyone else.'

Tizzie looked at the silly, beaming face of the puppet-woman; she lifted the string, and made the head nod up and down. None of this made any sense.

'So how long have *you* lived here?' she asked Davy.

'Two years – no, three. We came when I was nine. That's when my dad got his job here, then my gran as well.'

'Who gave them their jobs, then?'

Davy gave her an *isn't it obvious* look. 'Finnigan. Who else? He's in charge here.'

Tizzie frowned. 'I don't get it! This is Lord Rupert's house, and Greta's. But they've never been home, not once in three years. So where *are* they, then?'

'I think they're travelling abroad.' Davy was standing by the window, fiddling with the blind. He tweaked a cord, and the slats of the blind sprang apart to let in grey daylight; then he closed them again, and the room was theatrical in dark and light, as before. 'They're in Africa, or India or somewhere. Or perhaps it's Australia now. You'd have to ask

Finnigan. He's the only one who really knows.'

'I haven't met him yet,' Tizzie pointed out. 'When will I? He's the one who gave my mum her job, so it's a bit odd he hasn't come to meet her.'

Davy smiled. 'Finnigan *is* a bit odd. You'll see what I mean.'

'Odd how?'

'Wait and see.'

'He's not the only thing that's odd,' Tizzie retorted. 'This whole set-up is weird, if you ask me. What's the point of Lord Rupert owning this house at all, if he doesn't want to live here? He might as well sell it. It must be worth—' She hesitated, not really having any idea of house-prices, beyond the fact that she and Mum couldn't afford to rent one, let alone buy a house of their own. 'Thousands of pounds. *Hundreds* of thousands – millions, even—'

'Listen!' Davy cut in.

They both stood silent. *Creak, creak,* came the slow tread of footsteps along the corridor.

'It's him,' Davy said, close to her ear. 'Finnigan. You can ask him yourself.'

6
The Back Stairs

If she'd been on her own, Tizzie would have scuttled into the nearest hiding-place. But where? The room was empty, apart from the puppet-theatre, and it was too late to bolt out into the corridor. Besides, she was tingling with curiosity to see Finnigan.

The man who came in had grey hair and bristly eyebrows, and rimless glasses. He wasn't very tall; in fact he wasn't quite as tall as Davy. He walked in a tired, stooping way, and was all in brown: brown corduroy trousers, brown jacket with patched elbows, fawn pullover. Just inside the door he stopped abruptly, and fixed his eyes on Tizzie. Held in his gaze, she felt the force of his attention.

'Yes?' he said, as if she'd asked him a question.

'This is Tizzie,' Davy offered.

Only now did the man seem to notice that there was someone else in the room. His head swivelled round to look at Davy, then back at Tizzie.

'Tizzie? What kind of name is that?' His voice was cracked and husky.

'It's short for Elizabeth,' Tizzie told him.

'And what's brought you here, Tizzie-Elizabeth?'

Tizzie wasn't sure how to answer. Did he mean *here,* in this room? Or did he mean what had brought her to Roven Mere?

Davy spoke first. 'Her mum's the new cook.'

'Morag. Morag Furlong. That's her name,' Tizzie added, since Finnigan looked perplexed.

'Ah, yes,' he said, brightening. 'We've got a cook now. So she's arrived, has she? That's good. And you're her daughter.'

'I was just showing her round,' Davy explained.

'Good, good,' said Finnigan; then his eyebrows bristled together in a frown. 'Don't you go breaking anything, or moving things, though. Be sure to leave everything as you find it.'

'Course!' Davy sounded as if he'd been told this too many times to bother listening.

'Everything just as it is,' Finnigan repeated gruffly, more to himself than to anyone else. 'Everything in its proper place.'

He was carrying something slung over one shoulder: something black and stringy. Now, as he lowered it, Tizzie saw that it was another marionette, the figure of a man, thin as a stick-insect, dressed in a black suit and bow-tie. The face was stern, with neat black eyebrows and a twirled black moustache. This puppet looked more like the Finnigan of Tizzie's imagination than Finnigan himself did.

Suspending the puppet by the wooden cross-piece that held the strings, Finnigan began to make small movements with his fingers. At once the man-figure came to life. It stood on the floor, hands on hips, and turned its head to give Tizzie a stern look. Then it raised one arm and wagged a hand in warning. Almost, she could have believed that it pointed its finger, so expressive was the gesture.

'That's so clever!' She was enchanted. 'Did you make it?'

The puppet did a cheerful little dance, then was still. 'No, no,' said Finnigan. 'I only restore them. Give them new faces and clothes. I give them a new life.'

Tizzie's eyes were on the stick-man, now hanging limp from Finnigan's arm. 'Make it do some more! Please,' she remembered to add.

But Finnigan shook his head. 'They don't need me pulling their strings.' He lifted the marionette, and hung it up with the other two, in the puppet-theatre. 'Well, I must get on. Is it the weekend yet?' he asked Davy.

'Nearly,' said Davy. 'It's Friday.'

Finnigan nodded. 'I thought it was something like

that. So I'll see you tomorrow, in the workshop?'

'Course!'

Finnigan turned to Tizzie. 'You'd be most welcome to come too, if you've nothing better to do.'

'Thank you,' she said politely, with no idea where the workshop was, or what she might be expected to do there.

Pausing on his way out of the door, Finnigan said, 'Good day to you both.' Tizzie had the impression that he would have raised his hat if he'd been wearing one.

When she was quite sure he'd gone, she looked at Davy for a reaction. He was examining the new puppet, making it raise one foot and then the other.

'Well, I see what you mean – he *is* weird!' she remarked. 'Not knowing what day of the week it is! Is he all there?'

Davy looked at her, startled into anger; she saw the red flush rise in his cheeks. 'He's more all there than anyone I know!'

'I only meant—' said Tizzie, in dismay. 'I mean, *you* were the one who said he was odd—'

'Not the way you mean. Not like that,' Davy said. 'If you live like he does, one day's the same as any other. Why should he worry about what day it is?'

And he pushed past her, on his way out to the corridor.

'Wait!' Tizzie called. 'I'm sorry! Aren't we going to finish exploring?'

39

He turned again, quickly, but only to switch off the lights. 'Have you any idea how much electricity costs for a house this big, if people leave lights on all over the place? My gran's always reminding me.'

Tizzie had no idea at all. She tried again. 'Look, I'm really sorry. I didn't mean to be rude about Finnigan. Honestly I didn't! Can't we carry on exploring?'

'It can wait.'

The puppet-room was in darkness again. Tizzie was aghast: Davy was the first friend she'd begun to make here, and she'd spoiled things already! Wouldn't he believe that she was sorry? And she was; she really was. Why had she opened her mouth?

She expected Davy to head for the stairs they'd come up, but he turned along the corridor in the opposite direction.

'Where are you going, then?' she called after him.

'There's a different way back to the kitchen. I'll show you.'

He didn't slow down, didn't turn to see if she was following as she trotted along behind. She lost track of where they were going: along a corner, down five steps, across a landing, up again; then through a door to a dark flight of steps that wound and twisted several times before emerging at basement level.

Blinking and puffed, Tizzie recognised where she was. The stairs had brought her down to the farthest end of the kitchen corridor.

'Your mum's in there,' Davy told her as they reached the door to the kitchen. He carried on past.

He didn't say *Goodbye*, or *See you tomorrow*, or anything at all.

Now what would Tizzie say to Mrs Crump, who expected her and Davy to be such good friends?

Shamefaced, she sidled through the door. She found Mum deep in the larder, busy with labels and a marker-pen.

'Baking-powder, gelatine, vanilla essence,' she was muttering. 'Cream of tartar, ground almonds, glâcé cherries.'

With relief, Tizzie saw that Mum looked more cheerful than she'd been all day. Maybe she'd be happy now, with a big kitchen that was all hers.

'Well?' said Mum, seeing her. 'Have you been round the whole house?'

'No. Only part of it. But,' Tizzie said quickly, 'I met Finnigan!'

'Oh?' Mum paused, a jar of peaches in one hand.

'Yes, and he was really nice!' Tizzie rushed on, to make up for what she'd said to Davy. 'Do you know he makes puppets? String puppets? And he can make them work – he's really clever with them. He's got a workshop, and he—'

'Tizzie,' Mum said, looking at her hard, 'I don't want you talking to Finnigan more than you have to. He's a – he's a rather strange man. I don't think you should take much notice of what he says. And don't pester him.'

'But I—'

'Did you hear what I said?'

'I'm not deaf! You're only two feet away.' Tizzie had had enough. Why was everyone so unreasonable? *Be friends with this person, but not with that one. Don't ask questions, or you might hear the answers.*

And abruptly she felt close to tears.

7

The Blue Rowing-Boat

Waking to bright light through curtains, Tizzie couldn't at first remember where she was.

It was so quiet. Instead of busy traffic, she heard only birdsong, and the baaing of sheep. And the cottage itself was silent, unlike the block of flats in Tooting she and Mum had left yesterday morning. Was it really only yesterday? So much seemed to have happened since. There, besides the traffic in the busy street outside, she could always hear gurgling pipes, TV or radio from the adjoining flats, voices calling to each other, and the creak of footsteps from the floor above.

43

Tizzie felt as if she'd woken from a deep sleep, crowded with dreams she couldn't now remember.

It was Saturday. She did know that. Her first full day at Roven Mere. Less than a day she'd been here, and already she'd quarrelled with Davy.

Getting out of bed, she went to the window and opened the curtains. Yesterday's rain had cleared, and the day looked fresh, washed clean. She was looking out at the orchard: at the stunted but still graceful trees, at the path mown through long grass between them, and at woods and hedges and green fields as far along the valley as she could see. All was misted and still; it was the kind of day that would be hot later, when the sun emerged fully. She heard a pigeon cooing from the roof, and the scrabble of its claws on the slates.

Tizzie listened for movement from the room below, but there was none. Mum would still be asleep. She usually slept heavily, stirring just before seven, and then she would immediately be wide awake. Mum had no time for lingering in a dressing-gown while she drank tea and looked at the newspaper. She was always straight out of bed; showered, dressed and busy by the time Tizzie had properly woken up.

Today, for once, Tizzie would be up first: it was only just gone six. She dressed quickly in jeans and her yellow T-shirt and crept downstairs to the bathroom, then down again to let herself out of the front door.

The track from the main house, after leading

44

through the courtyard, continued past Cloud Cottage as far as a farm gate with a stile beside it, and a grassy path leading down the slope of the valley. It was an invitation Tizzie couldn't resist. She climbed the stile and walked on. How much of this land belonged to Roven Mere? To the bottom of the valley? Up the other side? All that she could see? She had no idea.

There was something quite intoxicating about being outside, alone, so early in the morning. It occurred to her that no one knew where she was, and maybe she should have left Mum a note; but she pushed the thought away, and strode along the path. It was of well-trodden grass; buttercups and longer grasses, beginning to flower, made dense borders on either side. Catching her breath at a sudden movement, Tizzie saw rabbits scampering for cover. Now, as the path rose to a brow of land, she could see right down to the bottom of the valley. A stream glinted between trees, then widened out into a lake, fringed with reeds.

Small lake or large pond, Tizzie wondered? Would there be fish? Ducks? Looking out, she saw a tiny island towards the far end – hardly more than a grassy knoll, with a shingle beach.

She had to go closer.

Her path led down the hillside at an angle, towards the grey roof of a building that squatted by the water's edge. Tizzie made her way down. The grass was longer here, and soaked with dew; her jeans soon clung to her legs, and her feet squelched inside her trainers.

The waterside building had no doors or windows that she could see. Picking her way around it, she saw that it was a boat-house, open-fronted and facing the lake. Inside, on struts in the water, was a wooden jetty; and tethered to that, bobbing slightly to the water's movement, was a small rowing-boat. It was painted in deep midnight-blue, with its name, *NEVERMORE,* painted in pale yellow on its prow. A pair of oars propped neatly over the stern were painted in the same dark blue.

Whose was it? Tizzie wondered. Lord Rupert's? Her feet loud on the planks of the jetty, she moved close enough to touch the boat's curving sides, to run her hand over the letters of its name. 'Nevermore,' she whispered aloud. 'Never more what?'

If she climbed into the rowing-boat, if she untied the rope that held it, if she lifted the oars and pushed off, away from the shelter of the boat-house, she could glide out on the lake like a girl in a fairy-story – someone tragic, someone misunderstood or betrayed, doomed to float for ever on the mirrored surface . . .

A loud quacking startled her into confusion: the flurry and panic of wings beating water. She sprang back guiltily from the boat as a shadow darkened the entrance.

A man. A man stood there, stooping under the low roof.

46

Tizzie lost her footing; she stumbled, then righted herself. The man was quite still, looking at her, blocking her way out.

It wasn't Finnigan; Tizzie took that in. This was an older man, shabbier. She registered a tanned unshaven face, stubbled in grey, and watery, blinking eyes.

What was she *doing* here? Why hadn't she stayed in bed? Now she'd be found dead and murdered, floating in the lake – strangled, beaten, or stabbed – killed by a madman! She let out a sob of fear. She was about to become a news headline: HUNT FOR MISSING GIRL. GIRL DROWNED.

There was a quick, bustly movement behind the man. A dog, a golden Labrador, pushed past him and surged up to Tizzie, wagging its tail, gazing at her face. The moment of stillness was broken, and the joyful-looking dog made her feel less scared.

The man hadn't moved. Now he swallowed audibly, seemed to struggle for words, and managed just one:

'Greta?'

'No! I'm Tizzie,' she told him. 'Excuse me.'

He stepped back, still gawping, as she sidled past him. Stumbling, the dog at her heels, she reached the path beside the boat-house and broke into a run, sprinting as fast as the uneven ground and the uphill slope allowed. The dog, whuffling happily, bounded behind.

'Hey! Come back here!' the man shouted, hoarse-voiced – whether to her or to his dog, she didn't wait to find out.

A quick glance back showed her that the dog had

47

stopped, caught in doubt; the man had stayed down by the lake shore, making no attempt to come after her. But she ran and ran until a stitch in her side doubled her up, and by that time – thankfully – she was within sight of Cloud Cottage.

8
Greta's Room

Once they'd had the chance to get shopping in, Mum told Tizzie, they'd have breakfast each morning at Cloud Cottage. Today, though, with nothing in their fridge apart from a carton of milk, they went up to the big kitchen in the main house for toast and cereal and orange juice. Their other meals – lunch and supper – would be eaten there as well, because Mum would be cooking for Finnigan and the staff. Eventually, when Lord Rupert came home, she'd cook for the family as well. Tizzie was impatient for the two weeks to go by. She was curious about the Evershalls, particularly Greta.

'*When* will they be coming home?' she asked Mum as they walked up through the courtyard and beside the yew hedge that bordered the track. 'Two weeks? Is that two weeks from today? Or is it less than that, now?'

'It might be soon,' said Mum. 'It might not be.'

'But Finnigan must *know*. Hasn't he told you? And why would he bother to get a cook, unless he's expecting them home?'

Mum tossed her head. 'Look, I told you Finnigan's a strange man. You can't believe everything he says.'

Tizzie hadn't told her mother anything about the other strange man, nor about her early-morning exploration. All she'd said, to explain away her wet jeans and the grass seed that clung to her trainers, was that she'd been out to look at the orchard. As Mum never bothered her with detailed questions, she could get away with things like that. Morag wasn't like Kamila's mum, who always had to know exactly where Kamila had been, and who with, and how long she had to wait for the bus, and who she'd seen on the way, and what homework she had and what marks she'd got. Tizzie was half-envious, and half not.

Today, Mum's lack of curiosity was useful, because all Tizzie needed to say was 'I'm going to look for Davy,' without mentioning where. As soon as they'd eaten their toast, Mum got to work: planning what to cook for lunch, and making a very long shopping-list.

Tizzie went outside and up the steps to the terrace. The gardens looked so different today, lush with growth and busy with bees. She smelled earth and greenness, and honeysuckle. Through an archway at the bottom of the terrace she saw a well-tended lawn, and climbing plants scrambling over a fence. She had never seen gardens quite like these – they were like different rooms or compartments, separated by walls, hedges or fences, with doors and arches leading from one to another.

While she stood hesitating, she saw Mrs Crump coming through the side gate, heading for the kitchen. She was dressed summerily, in a flowered dress that ballooned out over plump sandalled feet. Coral earrings dangled incongruously next to her square, mannish face.

'Bless you, lovey, you're up early!'

'Mum's in the kitchen,' Tizzie told her. Early? It felt as if half the morning had gone.

'Hard at work already, I bet. And what are you going to do with yourself today, dear? More exploring?'

'I was looking for Davy,' Tizzie said, hoping he hadn't told his gran that they'd parted on bad terms.

'Oh, he'll be helping Finnigan. He usually does, weekends.'

'Where's that?'

'Down in the workshop, over that way.' Mrs Crump made a vague gesture. 'Well, I must get on. You have fun, lovey.'

Tizzie set off in the direction indicated: down to the courtyard, then, at right-angles to the track that led to Cloud Cottage, she saw another, rutted and ill-kept, that headed off along the contour of the hillside towards a straggle of sheds or garages. Could that be it?

At first she thought she must have left the grounds of Roven Mere altogether; this area seemed so neglected and overgrown, after the mown lawns, tended flower-beds and neat paths of the garden. Nettles and brambles grew unchecked on each side of the track, and the buildings clustered ahead looked abandoned and ramshackle. An ancient caravan was parked nearby, wheel-less, resting on breeze blocks.

It was the kind of place where that man might loiter, the shabby man with the dog. She didn't want to bump into him again.

Deciding she'd make a mistake, Tizzie was about to turn back, and search the buildings of the courtyard instead. Then a voice called out, 'OK, I'll get it!' and Davy emerged from the largest of the sheds.

He stopped, seeing Tizzie; then waved and carried on.

'Davy!' she called to him. 'I've come to help in the workshop. I can, can't I? Is this it?'

'Yes, if you want. I'm just getting some tacks.'

He must have forgotten the bad feeling yesterday. Relieved, Tizzie followed him into a lean-to shed that adjoined the main one. It was a store-room for tools, but not the cluttery sort of place she expected. Instead, everything inside was in perfect order: hammers, saws and pliers hung on hooks, and there were shelves of cardboard boxes, each one labelled. It reminded her of Mum in the kitchen – everything that might be needed, everything in its place. Davy ran a finger along the highest shelf, reading the labels, until he came to '1cm tacks'. Reaching into the box, he took out a small packet.

As they turned back, Tizzie saw that the caravan door was open. Inside, she glimpsed a doormat, a padded bench, and a tiny table with a tea-pot and two mugs on it. A black cat was curled up, soundly asleep, on a green-checked cushion.

'Does someone live there?' Tizzie asked in a whisper.

'Course! Finnigan does.'

'But—' Tizzie was astonished. Finnigan was the most important person at Roven Mere: everyone kept saying so. He was in charge, the one who made decisions, the only person in touch with Lord Rupert. Tizzie had expected him to live in the house itself, in comfort. Not out here, like a tramp.

But, no, he didn't live like a tramp. One glance had shown her everything neat and clean, in contrast to the shabby exterior.

'Is this where he makes all the masks and things?'

'Come and see.'

Davy led the way into the workshop. Tizzie stood in the doorway, staring. There was too much to take in at one look. More puppets hung by their strings from a beam; paintings, and frames with no paintings in them, were stacked along one wall. A big wooden rocking-horse, dappled-grey with a red saddle and bridle, was frozen in mid-gallop. Hangings, embroidered and beaded and jewelled, were pinned to the walls. A pierrot face with blank black eyes stared down at Tizzie from a lofty height, next to another mysterious mask all stuck over with feathers. And in front of her, on a work-bench, stood a dolls' house. Its front doors, open wide, showed a bewildering number of rooms inside, fully furnished.

Having almost forgotten Finnigan in the wonder of her new surroundings, Tizzie was surprised when he scrambled stiffly up from the floor behind the dolls' house. In one hand he held a small hammer.

'Tizzie's come to help,' Davy told him, as he took no notice of her.

'Good, good,' said Finnigan, nodding. He held out his hand for the box of tacks.

Looking more closely at the dolls' house, Tizzie had the strange feeling that she knew it; that she'd been inside it. Then she realised that it was Roven Mere. She was looking at the rooms and corridors she'd roamed through yesterday afternoon, with Davy – she saw the dining-room, with three people seated at the long table; she saw the entrance hall and the stairs; on the upper floor there was a room with a replica of the puppet-theatre in it, and even minuscule puppets. If only she could shrink herself, like Alice in Wonderland, she could walk through the house, exploring all its rooms this time.

She studied the trio in the dining-room, paying close attention to the little figures. There was a man, a woman in an elegant green dress, and a fair-haired girl. The man was at the head of the table, the woman

54

to one side and the girl to the other; they occupied the three places set for them in the real room Tizzie had seen yesterday.

'Is this Lord and Lady Evershall, and Greta?' she asked.

Somehow it didn't feel right to say those names aloud. She hadn't been given permission.

Finnigan stopped what he was doing – tacking something to the floor in one of the back rooms – and appeared to consider her question very carefully before answering.

'Yes, indeed, Tizzie, you're quite right. That's exactly who they are.'

Moving her face as close as she could to the family group, Tizzie felt like a nosy giant. Lord Rupert wore a jacket and a bow-tie, and had neatly-parted dark hair. Lady Evershall – Tizzie had forgotten her first name, and didn't like to ask – was glamorous, with red lips and a pearl necklace. Most of all, Tizzie was interested in Greta, but the Greta-doll sat with her back to the outside, and it was hard to see her face. Her long hair was brushed back from her face and held in two slides. She wore a deep blue dress with a yellow sash.

On the table were plates crested with the letter 'E', in gold. There was a range of dishes and tureens, and knives and forks, and crystal glasses, and even tiny salt and pepper pots.

The father and the mother

were smiling; it was hard to see if Greta was, too.

She must be. They must be such a happy family. A spike of envy jabbed at Tizzie's chest.

When she looked up, she saw that Finnigan was watching her.

'What do you think?' he asked.

'I think Greta must be the happiest girl in the world,' she said.

'No. I meant what do you think of the dolls' house.'

'Oh, it's lovely. The best I've ever seen,' she told him shyly. That was certainly true. She could only remember seeing one other, in a museum. It had been far simpler than this, just a series of boxy rooms, and the doll-figures all out of proportion with the houses and with each other. Certainly not a perfect miniature, like this one.

'There's lots to do yet.' Finnigan stooped to look down at the kitchen; Tizzie wouldn't have been surprised to see a model Mum, sorting out cupboards, but the cook working there was large and smiley, in a frilled apron.

'We're laying carpet along the corridors,' Davy told her. He showed her a roll of maroon fabric on the bench, next to a measuring-tape, a ruler and a pair of scissors. 'It's a bit fiddly.'

'Now, let's find something for Tizzie to do,' said Finnigan. He walked once round the house, looking at it from all angles. 'Greta's bedroom needs curtains. Could you make those?'

'I don't know. I'll try.' Tizzie felt that her hands were too big and clumsy to do anything useful.

'Come and see,' Finnigan said, beckoning her round to the back of the house.

On the first floor, Greta's room was on the side of the house farthest from the main entrance: the side that, in reality, must face into the wooded slope of the hill. It would be a large room, though scaled down here to the size of a shoe-box. It had a white fire-place, a four-poster bed, a dressing-table and mirror. The open wardrobe door showed a rail of colourful clothes inside. On the wall were two paintings: one of a dappled-grey pony, the other a portrait of Greta (it must be!) in a blue dress, with hair brushed fair and shining over her shoulders. Again Tizzie peered closely, trying to see Greta's expression, but the portrait was too small – hardly bigger than her thumb-nail.

And, on a table by the window, stood a dolls' house – *this* dolls' house in miniature. Looking at it, Tizzie imagined a tiny Greta in there, about to eat her dinner with her parents. And *that* Greta would have a dolls' house in *her* room, even tinier. Tizzie imagined endless Gretas, endless dolls' houses, shrinking and shrinking to the point of disappearance. They whirled in her mind like water swooshing down a plughole.

'Now, fabric,' Finnigan was saying, sorting through a box on the bench. She hoped he might let her choose, but he'd already made his selection: of course, everything had to be just right. She smelled fresh cotton as he handed her a cut square: creamy yellow, patterned with dark blue flowers. 'This is the one. Scissors, pins, needles, thread, measuring-tape – all here.'

Tizzie set to work, measuring the windows. She wasn't much good at sewing, but it was a simple task to cut and hem the little curtains, and thread them on a rail. Carried away with her achievement, she made two matching cushions as well, stuffed with cotton-wool. Then Finnigan gave her three chair-pads, which had to be glued to their chairs.

They worked, the three of them, without talking much. Tizzie had countless questions to ask, but could tell that Finnigan wasn't a man who liked chatting. Still, it was companionable in the workshop, with only the occasional 'Pass the glue' or 'Hold this a minute' for conversation, and the tap-tapping of Finnigan's hammer. The black cat came in and played with a cotton-reel, batting it around the floor, before climbing into the fabric box and settling there to lick its paws. Every half-hour, a loud *cuckoo!* resounded, as a wooden bird burst through shutters on the Swiss clock above the bench, and clattered back in again.

'Will Greta be pleased?' Tizzie ventured, when the curtains were hung, looped back with silk thread, and the chairs all in place.

'I'm sure she'll be delighted,' said Finnigan.

'I can't wait for her to come home!' Tizzie couldn't help saying. 'When do you think it will be?'

'Oh – not so long now.' Finnigan busied himself

with tidying away the tools. 'Two weeks, maybe a bit more.' He looked up at the clock. 'That's enough for now. Lunchtime.'

Tizzie supposed that they'd all head up to Mum's kitchen, but Finnigan said he'd come later, and went into his caravan.

'But why does no one *know* about Lord Rupert?' Tizzie asked Davy, as they headed for the house. 'Not even Finnigan, and he's the one who's supposed to know everything?'

'It's just the way things are. It *is* a bit weird, but I suppose I've got used to it. But you know what?' Davy said. 'I wouldn't get yourself all excited about meeting Greta. I bet she's a spoilt little cow.'

9
The Well-House

Now it was Tizzie's turn to feel huffy and hurt. She stomped ahead, while Davy loitered to bash at stinging-nettles with a stick he'd picked up from the ground. Greta, spoilt and horrible! Of course she wasn't!

Greta was lonely, that was all. She could hardly help but be lonely, living in a huge place like this, with more rooms than she'd bothered to count. Tizzie imagined her roaming the house and gardens – knowing that she ought to be happy, but missing something important. Greta lived in unbelievable luxury, but what she lacked was a *friend*.

What she lacked was Tizzie. Tizzie felt quite sure of that.

How delighted Greta would be, when she arrived home to find that there was a girl her own age living at Roven Mere, a girl ready and willing to be her friend! Tizzie's mind soared. They'd explore together, they'd venture into attics and up every twisty staircase. They'd go out into the fields and woods: they'd pick flowers and blackberries, they'd climb trees, they'd have special secret places that no one else knew.

Having almost forgotten that it was a story she was telling herself, Tizzie was annoyed now with Davy, for spoiling it. It wasn't as if he even *knew* Greta, was it? No one did, only Finnigan. And Finnigan would hardly spend hours making a dolls' house for her, would he, if he knew her as spoilt and pampered?

Her irate march had brought her to the top of the kitchen steps. Here she stopped dead, seeing a golden Labrador tethered to a wall-ring by the lower door. Seeing her, it gave a friendly *whuff.* She'd forgotten all about her encounter by the lake this morning. The newspaper headlines slammed into her mind again: GIRL MISSING, GIRL FOUND DROWNED. But if that man was having lunch, then of course he wasn't a murderer after all, but someone who worked here.

Feeling foolish, she went down and in. The kitchen smelled of warm bread and herbs; Mrs Crump was sitting at the long table, with the dog-man, and another younger man Tizzie hadn't seen before. Mum was bringing a jug of water from the fridge. She looked flushed, almost pretty, the way she only did when she was cooking or serving food. Mrs Crump was serving herself with a slice of quiche; both men were already eating hungrily.

'Oh, and here's Tizzie.' Mrs Crump flashed her a big smile. 'Have you had a nice morning, dear? Don't suppose you've met Jack Doughty, have you? And this is Will, Davy's dad.'

'Hello,' Tizzie said shyly.

'Pleased to meet you, Tizzie,' said Will Crump. He had a tanned, smiley face, and hair that was just as thick, though not so long, as Davy's. He was handsome, in a careless sort of way. Jack Doughty nodded at Tizzie and said something like, 'Ar, oh.' He made no comment about seeing her by the boat-house. Now that she saw him in more ordinary surroundings, he didn't look frightening after all. He was just an old man, with a mild expression, and filmy blue eyes that looked at her rather vaguely.

'There'll be more of us here weekdays, when the cleaners are in,' said Mrs Crump, 'but course you'll be at school.'

School! Tizzie didn't want to start thinking about that.

'Speaking of school,' Mum said, sitting at the end of the table, 'we'll get your uniform this afternoon. Mrs Crump knows a woman who sells it second-hand. She's in the next village – we'll go there as soon as I've cleared away.'

'OK,' Tizzie said, with a sense of foreboding. She sat in the place next to Mrs Crump, who cut her a large piece of quiche. There were sausage-rolls as well, and salad, and bread warm from the oven. For a few moments everyone continued eating, in the sort of silence that meant the food was too good to be interrupted with talk. Mum, as usual, had put only a small amount on her own plate, and picked at it in a bored way. She liked cooking more than she liked eating.

Jack Doughty waved a piece of bread in Tizzie's direction, and said, 'Lovely cook, your mum is. You learn to cook like she does, you won't have any trouble finding a husband.'

Tizzie had no idea what he meant – only that *Mum* hadn't got a husband, had never had one, and didn't want one now. Mrs Crump coughed awkwardly; Mum shrugged, as if the remark wasn't worth answering.

'Here's Davy now,' said Mrs Crump. 'Come on, love. You must be ravenous.'

'Never learned to cook, I didn't,' said Will. 'Good tactic, that. Means someone else always has to do it for me.'

'That's just being lazy,' Mum retorted, in her forthright way. 'Cooking's not *difficult*. Just a matter of following instructions. Anyone can read a recipe.'

'Yes, but it takes that special touch.' Jack Doughty reached for the bread-board. 'That's the magic ingredient. And you've got that, all right.'

He thought I was Greta, Tizzie remembered, wondering. Then, she hadn't seen Greta: but by now, with the doll and the portrait in mind, she wondered how he could have made such a mistake. She and Greta were both girls, that was the main and only resemblance. But Greta's hair was long and blonde and sleek, not carroty and wild like Tizzie's. Greta was taller and slimmer, and her eyes, unlike Tizzie's sludge-coloured ones, were blue. Tizzie didn't know how she knew these things, but she felt sure she did. Almost, she could feel Greta looking at her; she could hear her voice saying, 'Tizzie! Where've you been, all this time?'

Now Finnigan came in, nodded at everyone and sat at the far end of the table. He served himself with food, ate it quickly without joining in the conversation, and got up to go as soon as he'd finished. 'Thank you, Morag – that was delicious,' he said gruffly to Mum.

'It wasn't much,' Mum answered, offhand. Davy left, too, while the others stayed for fruit and coffee. Tizzie took an apple from the bowl, deciding to follow Finnigan and Davy back down to the workshop.

'Three o'clock, back here,' Mum told her. Tizzie nodded and went up the steps, biting into her apple.

Thinking she'd try a different way through the gardens, she turned right along the terrace and went through a brick arch. There was a paved walk here, and a formal lily-pond with a fountain in the shape of a leaping fish that spouted an arc of water from its mouth. Then a second identical archway. Tizzie knew that she'd need to turn left down the slope to reach the workshop, but through the arch she stopped to look at what seemed to be a new garden, a garden-in-progress. It was thickly hedged in yew, with four small square beds dug over and ready, but with nothing planted in them. The lawn looked sparse, freshly-seeded. A wheelbarrow stood in the centre, with a fork and a spade lying across it. At the far end, wide steps led up to a paved area.

Davy's dad must be working here, Tizzie supposed. There was no way out at the end, and the yew hedge was too thick to squeeze through, so she retraced her steps to the lily-pond, and found steps leading down to the next level. From here, she saw her way to the line of trees and the picket-fence that marked the lower edge of the garden.

A whistle sounded to her left, piercing and shrill, like someone giving signals to a sheep-dog. Looking that way, Tizzie saw an open-sided building, really nothing more than a roof on struts. In its centre was a circular structure, a well, perhaps. She picked her way along the flagged path between flower-beds. It was Davy who'd whistled; he was coming from the other side, along a rose-walk.

She thought at first that the well was just an ornamental one, but now saw that it was too solid for that. Its wall was as high as her chest, made of brick capped with concrete. Iron struts stood either side, supporting a winding mechanism: there was no bucket, but a chain and hook to hang one on.

'Is it a real well?' Tizzie said, looking in. Brickwork,

with fronds of fern clinging to its cracks, plunged into darkness. A long, long way down, she saw the faintest glimmer of light on water, and smelled the cold weedy dankness. It was like looking into a dark porthole. Feeling giddy, she straightened up rather quickly. 'Yes, it is! I can see water at the bottom!'

'Course it's real,' said Davy. 'It's how Roven Mere got its water, ages ago before there was taps and plumbing.'

Tizzie was still holding her apple-core. She held it out over the dark drop and let it fall. Listening intently, she heard the faintest plop into water, a good few seconds later. 'You could fall down there and never get out.' Immediately she wished she hadn't said it, letting him know he'd scared her. Maybe he'd only brought her here to give her a fright, so that he could jeer about it for ever after. Tizzie had met plenty of boys like that. Girls, too. People who wanted to pick on her and make her look stupid, just because she was new.

But Davy laughed – not in an unkind way – and said, 'Don't look down, then, if it makes you feel weird.'

'Aren't you going back to the workshop?' Tizzie asked him.

'Might do, later. Finnigan usually has a nap after lunch.'

'In his caravan?'

'Course. Where else?'

'You'd think – you know, with all those empty rooms in the house – Lord Rupert would have given

Finnigan a nice room of his own. It must be lonely down there by himself.' Tizzie thought of dark winter nights, and winds battering the little caravan. How flimsy it must feel, inside!

'It's what Finnigan likes. He's OK. He's got Small.'

'Small?'

'His cat.'

Only now did Tizzie remember that she'd meant to be cool with him for what he'd said about Greta, but this went quite out of her head when Davy said, 'Is your mum on her own, then? Haven't you got a dad?'

'Not really.' She turned to look back into the well.

'Where is he? Do you ever see him?'

'I've *never* seen him, not once. He's never been around. I don't know much about him. Only his name.'

'Yeah?'

'Michael Rafferty. He's Irish.'

'He would be, with a name like that. Sounds like someone in a song. There's one my dad sings sometimes, *Rafferty's Motor-Car.*'

He began to hum. He had an awful, tuneless voice.

Into Tizzie's mind floated a picture of how her life might have been, with a dad in it. She saw Mum and herself in an open-topped car, with Michael Rafferty at the wheel, singing. They'd be in Ireland. Tizzie was hazy about what Ireland might look like, but she'd seen a holiday advert on TV, once, showing a road through mountains, and lots of green. They could be there in that picture, the three of them. They'd be smiling and happy, and Michael Rafferty's rust-coloured hair would be tousled by the wind. That was one of the few things she knew about him: his hair was rusty-red, like hers. Mum said it was from him that Tizzie got her carroty hair. Mum also said that he had a voice that could charm the birds out of the trees.

Kamila had said, once, 'Your mum might meet someone new. Someone nice.' A boyfriend, she meant. Possibly even a step-dad for Tizzie. No! Tizzie didn't want that. She was used to just Mum and her, however irritating or frustrating Mum could be. Mum sometimes had boyfriends, without seeming to care much whether she did or not; she moved somewhere new, or dumped them, or drove them away with her snappishness, before they'd been around for long. But somewhere in the background – forever young, forever handsome and charming – was the father called Michael Rafferty.

'What about you?' Tizzie said, to deflect the conversation from herself. 'Haven't you got a mum?'

'Had,' said Davy. 'She died. When I was nine. She got ill and died.'

'Oh. Sorry.' Tizzie didn't know what else to say, because while Davy was speaking his mouth had gone twisty and his voice had wobbled.

Davy turned away from her. With one hand on the iron support, he climbed on to the rim of the well and stood upright there; then he leaned perilously over the long, darkening drop.

Tizzie's thoughts blurred in panic. 'No!'

'It's all right! I'm not going to jump in. Had you worried, though, didn't I?' He was smiling now. He lowered himself to sit on the concrete coping, his legs dangling inside.

Any minute now, she thought, he'd dare her to do the same. He might want to get back at her, because she'd almost seen him cry. Well, she wouldn't do it. He could jeer if he liked.

With his fingernail, Davy prised a clump of green moss away from the brickwork, and held it in his fingers to examine it. 'So,' he said. 'This Michael Rafferty, does he even know you exist?'

'I don't know. I suppose he doesn't.'

'He might have a whole nother family of his own. He might be married with children.'

This was so obvious that Tizzie couldn't think why she'd never thought of it for herself. Immediately, she hated the idea. She wanted Michael Rafferty to be *her* father, and no one else's.

'I'm going now,' she told Davy, turning away. 'Mum's taking me to get school uniform.'

It was only when she was in the van with Mum, driving out through the gates and uphill to the village, that something occurred to her.

What if Mum married Davy's dad? Wouldn't that make two bits of families into a complete one?

Tizzie resolved to look more closely at Will Crump, next time she saw him. Did she want him as a step-dad? Did she want Davy as a step-*brother*?

And had Mum thought of this – had she *known* about Will? Met him, perhaps, when she came for the interview? Tizzie glanced at her, sidelong. Could Will be the reason for Mum coming to Roven Mere?

10
The Oak Wardrobe

Debbie Green, the woman who ran the school uniform exchange, lived in a cottage in the next village, Upper Sleet. She kept her stores in a garage, on rails and in boxes. Soon Tizzie was kitted out with a maroon sweatshirt, two white shirts, a maroon-and-silver tie, and a grey wrap skirt.

'Your old PE kit'll have to do for now,' Mum said, frowning at the items on display. 'I don't get paid till the end of the week.'

Debbie had a daughter called Robin, who was in Year Seven, the same as Tizzie. Robin − small and neat, with straight dark hair − told Tizzie that she'd be on the same bus every morning. 'That'll be good. It's only boys, otherwise, from this village and yours. You might even be in my form.'

Robin seemed nice, and Tizzie was glad that she'd now know *two* people on the school bus. But on the drive back to Roven Mere, her mind turned to the friend she most wanted to meet: Greta.

'Do you think Greta will go to the same school?' she asked Mum.

'*What?*'

'Greta! Lord Rupert's daughter!' Greta was so much in her thoughts that Tizzie expected Mum to be thinking of her as well.

'No. I don't think so.'

'But she must go to school *some*where. How's she been allowed to miss so much, being away so long?'

'How should I know? She'd go to a posh private school. Maybe her father pays for a private tutor.'

Tizzie fell silent. Of course, Greta wouldn't be likely to attend the local comprehensive, or go there on the bus with children from the village. And Greta would have friends of her own; or, if she didn't, she'd soon make new ones. Posh friends from her posh school.

'Is Lord Rupert very rich, then?'

'He seems to have so much money, he doesn't know what to do with it.' Mum sounded cross.

'Don't you like him?'

'How do I know whether I like him or not? Does it matter?'

'I'd have thought it matters quite a lot!'

'Well,' said Mum, slowing for the bend by the village shop, 'maybe I will, maybe I won't. I'm not going to like him just because he's rich.'

'No, I didn't mean—' Tizzie tried again. 'When you said Finnigan was in charge here, I thought you meant he sat in an office doing accounts and stuff, or walked round checking up on everyone. Do you know he spends all his time making things for Greta? That must be Lord Rupert's orders, mustn't it?'

'Everything that happens here is on Lord Rupert's orders.'

'And the others – do you like them? Finnigan and Mrs Crump? And – Will?'

Mum only shrugged. 'They're OK. I hardly know them.' They'd come swooshing down the lane where it curved sharply past the trees; now Mum pulled up at the gates. Just as she'd done yesterday, Tizzie got down to open them, and waited while Mum drove through.

How different Roven Mere looked now from the bleak, rain-lashed facade it had presented yesterday! Now, in warm sunshine, with the trees stirred by the faintest of breezes, the house seemed perfectly positioned on its hillside, sheltered by the trees above, and looking down over its secret gardens. The shutters had been opened today, giving the house a kindlier appearance. Still, Tizzie was glad she lived in Cloud Cottage, not in the empty splendour of the mansion.

Mum parked the van outside the cottage. Tizzie put the new clothes away in her wardrobe, while

Mum went back to the main house to start preparing the evening meal.

Tizzie had a plan. She went to the kitchen with Mum, and drank a glass of squash. Then, when she was quite sure that no one was around, and Mum occupied with chopping onions and peppers, she slipped out into the corridor and up the twisty back stairs.

Having looked at the dolls' house this morning, she now had a mental map of the house, a better one than yesterday's exploration with Davy had given her. She hadn't yet been on the first floor, where the bedrooms were, but she counted her way up through the landings and turns, and pushed open the second door she came to. As she'd expected, when she closed it behind her it was flush against the wood panelling, as nearly invisible as the one she'd gone through with Davy into the room-between-rooms on the ground floor.

She glanced in both directions to check that no one was coming. All was quiet. She was standing in a wide corridor, with windows on one side and doors along the other. The floor was thickly carpeted in moss green, allowing her to tread silently. By each window stood a small table with a tasselled cloth and a vase of fresh flowers.

Tizzie made her way along, cautiously, as there was nowhere to hide unless she darted into one of the rooms – and the doors might be locked. Ahead, she could see the windowed panel that led through to the main stairs. The corridor turned left here;

she'd need to go that way to reach Greta's room.

She had memorised its position from the dolls' house. When the corridor turned left again, she counted the doors until she reached the fifth. This door, like all the others, was white and panelled, with a large brass handle. Here she stopped, undecided. She needn't go in: she could go downstairs and forget all about it, go and find Davy. But she was here now, and might not have a better chance; there would be more staff around if she came back on a weekday.

Grasping the handle, she turned it and pushed gently.

She was looking into the room she'd seen in the dolls' house. She stepped inside, and closed the door behind her.

There it all was: the four-poster bed, the curtains she almost felt she'd made herself, the fireplace, wardrobe, dressing-table and mirror. By the window stood the long table where the dolls' house would go, now occupied by a vase of roses in bud. Surely those roses, so fresh, could only have been put here this morning, Tizzie thought, with the anxious feeling that she was about to be caught. What could she possibly say? What excuse could she find for being in Greta's room? At least, here, there were possible hiding-places. If she heard someone coming, she could crawl under the bed. It was big enough for six people to hide under there, and the bedspread fell all the way to the floor.

Another door opened into a little bathroom, all in

white, with dark blue towels on a rail and a new bar of soap in a holder. A deep blue dressing-gown hung on a hook. What amazing luxury! Everything was ready for Greta to come home.

And there was the portrait. This was what Tizzie most wanted to see.

The two paintings were hung one each side of the door, as in the dolls' house. One was of the pony, with its plumed white tail and its bold gaze. The other was of Greta, looking down from her frame.

'Hello, Greta,' Tizzie whispered.

Greta's lips were slightly parted, as if she were about to reply. Her hair was brushed and shining, held back from her face in an Alice band, then falling over her shoulders. She wore a dress of deep blue, with short sleeves, and a cream lace collar and cuffs. She sat with her back to an open window, with summer trees beyond; it was, Tizzie realised, *this* window. Greta had posed for the portrait here, in her bedroom.

Tizzie moved around the room, touching a brush and comb on the dressing-table, a small mirror, a mosaic box, a china pony. Everything was dusted and polished. Who came in here? Who looked after Greta's things?

When Tizzie looked back at the portrait she felt she was looking at the face of a friend. Davy had got it wrong about Greta, she was sure; but then, of course, he didn't know her. He was just supposing – but getting it all wrong. If he saw Greta's picture he would know, as Tizzie did, that Greta was funny and kind, nice to be with. She would love sharing secrets and jokes. She'd be very good at inventing games, complicated ones that involved hiding in secret parts of the house, and dressing up in costumes.

The oak wardrobe stood by the wall opposite the bed, tall and wide, but unlike the one in the dolls' house its doors were closed, with a little round key in the lock. As soon as Tizzie had the idea of looking inside, it was irresistible. The key clicked as it turned, then the door swung open with a whining creak. Tizzie froze for a moment, but no one burst in to confront her.

She stared and stared: she reached out a hand and touched a beaded sleeve, a velvet skirt. Greta had even more clothes than Kamila! There were dresses and coats, jeans and tops and skirts: far more than Tizzie and Mum owned between them, more than Tizzie ever expected to have in the whole of her life.

'Oh, Greta!' she whispered aloud.

They weren't exactly Tizzie's kind of clothes – the fabrics, colours and styles, even at a glance, were somehow different – but of course Greta was a rich girl, and probably went to expensive shops. Underneath, there was a rack of shoes and boots, all clean and polished. Tizzie didn't dare to look any more closely.

And these were only the clothes Greta had left behind! She must have others with her – her favourites, probably. Tizzie imagined Greta as a traveller in an old-fashioned story or film, taking huge amounts of luggage with her, a weighty trunk perhaps, which would have to be wheeled around by a porter. And Greta had been away for so long – *how* long, exactly? – that she'd have grown out of her old clothes, and would have needed to buy new ones. But these garments looked as if they'd fit Tizzie.

The thought was just creeping into her mind that surely no one would notice if she borrowed some of these clothes, when a silky blue fabric caught her attention. Tentatively, she stretched out her hand, and touched it.

It was a dress, deep blue, lustrous, with a cream lace collar and cuffs. It was the dress worn by Greta in the portrait. A *girly* dress, a party kind of dress, for some special occasion, maybe. Or perhaps it had been bought specially for the portrait.

Carefully, Tizzie lifted it down from the rail. She held it against herself: it seemed to be just her size. She smoothed the fabric against her, and did a twirl. At once she wanted to put the dress on: but now her nerve failed her. She hung it back in its place, closed the wardrobe door very gently, trying not to let it squeak, and turned the key.

As she moved to the dressing-table, she caught sight of her own reflection in the mirror and jumped back in alarm. Beginning to feel dizzy, she sat on a cushioned stool and slid open one of the small dressing-table drawers. Inside there were shiny, sparkly things: neck-laces, bangles and hair-slides. Tizzie was about to take out a slide and try it in her hair when she met her own reflected eyes again. So guilty she looked, so furtive! Nothing like the sleek and pampered Greta in the portrait.

'You shouldn't be here,' Tizzie whispered to the girl in the mirror. What if someone came in and found her? What if someone brought more flowers, or came in to dust? What excuse could she possibly have?

Only the truth. *I just wanted to look,* she could say. *I wanted to see Greta's things.*

She peeped out carefully into the corridor, both ways, before slipping through, and closing Greta's door behind her.

11

The Grandfather Clock

Very early next morning, Tizzie lay awake in bed, puzzling. Things didn't make sense.

Greta was the same age as Davy and herself, Mrs Crump had said: twelve (which Tizzie wasn't quite, yet). As Greta hadn't been at home for at least three years – the three years Davy had lived here – she couldn't have been more than nine when she left. But the Greta in the portrait was the Greta Tizzie had imagined, the friend of her own age; and the dress in the wardrobe was the right size for Tizzie. Tizzie wasn't big or tall for her age, but she was surely bigger than most girls of nine.

Then the portrait! Since Greta as shown was clearly eleven or twelve, it couldn't have been painted here. At first Tizzie thought that it must have been done in India, or Africa, or Australia, or wherever Greta was, and sent on home. But that didn't add up, either. Tizzie had recognised the window in Greta's bedroom, the trees and the hillside behind.

Maybe the artist in India (or Africa, or Australia . . .) had only imagined the details of home, or had painted them from memory? That wouldn't be impossible. Probably Greta felt homesick, and this portrait reminded her of Roven Mere? In that case, though, wouldn't she want to keep the painting with her? Instead, it had been sent on home – and the dress with it.

The fact remained that Greta hadn't been here for at least three years. The room Tizzie had stood in had belonged to a younger Greta; yet it was the girl in the portrait, the funny friend, the secret-sharer, the bedroom-giggler, that Tizzie had sensed there. She could see Greta's face now, as if they had known each other for ages.

If only Greta would come back! Then all these mysteries could be sorted out. There would be some simple explanation.

Meanwhile, the only person who knew the answers was Finnigan. She would have to ask him, in spite of what Mum said.

After breakfast, Tizzie headed down to the work-shop. She expected to find Davy there, but instead

Finnigan was on his own. Two drab-looking puppets hung on hooks on the wall, with faded faces, tangled strings, and tattered clothes. One was meant to be a clown, with eyebrows that shot up in great arcs of surprise, and a mouth shaped like a banana. The other was so faded that it seemed to have no face at all.

'They need new strings,' Finnigan said when he saw Tizzie – no *hello*, no *how are you today*: it was just as if they were picking up where they'd left off yesterday – 'as well as new clothes and new faces.'

'New lives,' said Tizzie.

'That's right.' He looked at her. 'Can you paint? Could you do the faces?'

'I can try,' Tizzie said. 'But what sort of faces do you want?'

'I—' Finnigan began, then appeared to reconsider, and said, 'You decide.' He sorted out paints for her, and brushes; water in a jam-jar, and a saucer for mixing.

Today he was mending a grandfather clock. He had laid it on its back along the bench like a patient on an operating table, and had spread tiny cogs and wheels and screwdrivers all over the bench. Small, the black cat, perched on the edge, occasionally dabbing a paw at one of the clock parts.

Looking at the faceless puppet, Tizzie thought of turning it into Greta. But no, that was too hard; already, when she tried to fix Greta's face in her mind, it blurred, and swam out of focus. She opened a jar of paint, and another, and began to mix colours in the saucer.

'Two weeks, did you say, before Lord Rupert comes home?' she remarked, as casually as she could.

'Oh, something like that,' Finnigan replied, bent close over the work-bench.

'But *when,* then?'

'Soon. Some time soon, it'll be.'

Tizzie knew how vague adults could be when they wanted to avoid giving a proper answer. What she wanted was a definite date.

'But how will you *know*? Will he phone? Write a letter? Send an email?'

'Lord Rupert will let me know of his plans,' Finnigan said.

The mildness of his manner made her feel bold enough to persist. 'Is he nice? Do you like working for him?'

'Yes, I'm happy in my work, as happy as I could be. It's kind of you to ask, my dear.' Finnigan gave her an odd sideways look, as if he'd never considered the matter before. 'Lord Rupert, I hope, is a very fair employer.'

'What's he like?'

'That, Tizzie, you must decide for yourself.'

'But when can I?'

'Soon, when Lord Rupert comes home.'

'And Greta?' Tizzie went on, with a flush of embarrassment in case Finnigan could tell that she'd been prying in Greta's room. 'What's she like?'

'Ah,' said Finnigan. 'If only I could tell you that. Let me tell you a story instead.'

'A story? Your story? One you've made up?'
'Just a story,' said Finnigan. 'It goes like this.

Once there was a man who wanted to know what happiness was, and how to find it.

Who should he ask? Who would know? First, he asked a very wealthy man. 'Happiness is money, and lots of it,' was the answer, 'for I can buy anything I want, ten times over.' But Peregrine – that was his name – wasn't satisfied with that, for money can only be spent, and then it is gone. Next he went and looked for the most beautiful woman he could find, and asked her the same question. 'To be beautiful is to be happy,' said the lovely lady; 'for I know that everyone who looks at me is glad.' But Peregrine didn't believe that either, for beauty fades and withers like the petals of a rose. So he went on his way again, and came to a troupe of actors performing in the cathedral square. At the end of their performance, everyone clapped and cheered. Peregrine waylaid the lead actor, and asked him the same question: What is happiness? 'Happiness, good sir,' said the actor, 'is fame.' But Peregrine didn't think that could be true, for fame is like a bubble, swelling and swelling with its own importance until it bursts and is gone. So off he went once more.

He roamed around the city, asking everyone he came

across, but could find no answer that pleased him. From a lover, gathering forget-me-nots for his sweetheart – 'Happiness is being in love.' Peregrine considered that, but decided that love is usually selfish, and passed by. To the poacher, slinking out of a gateway with a brace of rabbits – 'Happiness is a good shot.' But the poacher's happy shot brought death to the rabbits; Peregrine shook his head, and walked on in search of more answers. To the old, happiness could only be found in youth; to the sick, happiness could only be found in a return to health; to the labourer, happiness would be in idleness; to the man without work, happiness would lie in honest toil.

Peregrine thought and thought, and concluded that true happiness can only be found in _un_happiness, for he had met only people whose happiness was not recognised until lost, or people who thought that happiness was theirs by right, not foreseeing how soon it would pop like a balloon. And that made him miserable, for happiness, it seemed, could never truly be found; or if found, could certainly never be kept.

So, despairing of ever finding an answer, he left the town, and walked along a country lane. Passing a farmstead, he saw a pig-man cleaning out a sty. I should have said, he _smelled_ the farmstead before he saw it; for the pigman was shovelling manure and soaked straw that had lain in the sties for weeks. The smell, riper and pongier than old socks, wafted along the lane and hung in the air like smog. It filled Peregrine's nose until he was sure that he must reek of pig himself.

Dusk was beginning to fall now, and Peregrine hastening on his way to the next town to find lodging for the night. So when the pigman raised his cap and said, 'Good evening to you, sir,' Peregrine merely said 'Good evening' in return, and passed by. But then he thought, 'Why should I not ask this fellow the same question? His opinion is as worth having as anyone else's.'

So he retraced his steps, and this about-face turned him towards the setting sun. 'Excuse me, good sir,' he said to the pig-man. 'What, in your view, is happiness?'

The pig-man had been about to empty a bucket of stinking slops into the road. He looked perplexed at the question. While he considered how to answer, he hoisted his bucket, and chucked its contents over the wall of the sty. Just for an instant, the rank water hung in the air in separate drops, and each drop caught the golden radiance of the sunset in a shimmering fall that lasted for maybe one second. Peregrine gasped in admiration. Then the droplets fell to the ground to mingle with the mud and dirt there.

The pig-man grinned. 'There's your answer,' he said. 'Happiness is a moment that comes and is gone.'

'But gone so quickly!' said Peregrine.

'Ay,' said the pig-man, 'and there's the beauty of it. Moments like that, you keep them in your mind. They're like pearls threaded on a string.'

Peregrine thanked him, and went on his way. He was glad, for this humble pig-man had shown him what no one else could. Now his mind was full of pig-slurry turned to gold, for just a moment, a glorious moment. A moment of pure happiness. A pearl on the string of his life.'

Finnigan stopped talking, and looked at Tizzie for a reaction.

'Is that it?' she said. 'The end?'

'Yes, I think so.' While he'd been telling the story, Finnigan had put the grandfather clock together and closed its door. Now he tipped it upright, and held it till he was sure it was quite steady on its feet. Tizzie heard a steady, deep ticking.

She was disappointed. 'I thought Greta was going to come into the story. But it wasn't about Greta at all.'

'I didn't say it would be,' said Finnigan. 'It was just a story.'

'Did you make it up?'

'Well, that's something you never really know, with stories.' Finnigan was cleaning the glass of the clock-face. 'They just come, and you don't know quite where from.'

'My father was a storyteller,' Tizzie told him.

Finnigan looked at her. 'Was, Tizzie?'

'Oh, I don't mean he's died or anything like that. Not that I know, anyway. It's just, I've never met him.

Mum didn't know him for long, either. She had a summer job picking fruit on a farm, in Kent I think it was, and so did he. Michael Rafferty, that's his name. He had gingery hair like mine, and he told stories, wonderful stories.' Tizzie paused: it was hard to imagine Mum, a younger Mum – well, not actually a mum at all, back then – who liked stories, who would bother to listen, who wouldn't have more important things to do with her time. Tizzie pictured Mum sitting on the ground by a camp-fire at the edge of a strawberry field, hugging her knees, her eyes fixed on the face (a face Tizzie couldn't make herself see at all clearly – only the hair) of Michael Rafferty. Michael Rafferty's voice would tell of questions and answers, heroes and villains, riddles and solutions. And because Tizzie so liked the phrase Mum had used, *he had a voice to charm the birds out of the trees,* she couldn't help imagining them: blackbirds and robins, rooks and crows, perched on the ground and on nearby bushes and fences, to listen too. 'That's about all I know,' she added, as Finnigan was looking at her, as if expecting more.

He nodded. 'Two good things, then. Autumn hair, and the art of telling tales. Has he passed his gift on to you, Tizzie, along with the hair?'

'I don't know. I like stories, but I don't think I'm much good at making them up. I liked yours,' she added politely.

'Thank you.' Finnigan gave a little bow.

'It was sad, though.'

'Was it?' said Finnigan.

'Yes! A sad story about happiness.'

'But maybe it was a happy story about sadness? Now,' said Finnigan, collecting together his screw-drivers and pliers, putting each item in its special place in his toolbox, 'tell me about this face you've been painting. Who is this person?'

Tizzie looked critically at the puppet. She'd been trying to make it look like Nannina, but now its features were smeared and lopsided, like a clumsy drawing done by a child. 'It hasn't come out like I wanted. I think I'll leave it for now, and start again tomorrow.'

12

The Wobbly Stile

On Monday morning, Tizzie, in her second-hand uniform, walked with Davy up to the village bus-stop.

Davy had come down from Mere Lodge to meet her, this first day. They set off along the entrance drive, but instead of walking as far as the road, Davy turned through a small gate that led to a footpath. This path made a steep diagonal across a grass meadow, and then through trees, joining the lane as it wound up to the village. There was a stile to be climbed, a stile that had a wobbly cross-piece. Davy went over first; then, as Tizzie balanced on top, she heard a shout, and saw two boys coming along the road.

'That's Lee and Tim Dingleby,' Davy told her. 'They live at Mill Farm.'

Both boys were tall and skinny, with dark floppy hair. Tim was much older, probably year ten or eleven; he was listening to an iPod, so just smiled vaguely and went on up the hill. Lee, as soon as he heard Tizzie's name, pranced round her, grinning, tugging at her rucksack: 'Don't get into a tizzy, Tizzie!'

Tizzie rolled her eyes. Did he really think she'd never heard that before? Did he think it was amazingly witty? But Davy laughed, too, and got involved in a silly kicking-and-scuffing game with Lee. Tizzie put on an aloof air, and walked on uphill behind Tim.

They were only just in time. The bus came round the corner and stopped outside the pub; two more boys came running. Boarding, Tizzie explained to the driver – as instructed by Mrs Crump – that she had no bus pass yet, but would get one from the school office later. Then she saw someone waving from the back seat. Robin. Relieved to get away from the boys, Tizzie went to sit next to her.

Soon the bus had left the fields and villages behind, and was on the edge of a large-ish town. Tizzie felt more at home here, looking out at rows of shops, a sports centre, and estates of ordinary houses.

She was used to finding her way around new schools, facing the confusion of timetables and teachers, groups and sets, corridors and labs and gyms, and to not minding very much if things were confusing. Her survival tactic was to fade into the background. Always, whatever class she was in, she'd try to find a place at the back where she could hide behind a bigger person, staying out of the teacher's line of view. She rarely got into trouble, and never willingly drew attention to herself; she wasn't especially clever, nor especially stupid, so could get by in most lessons. Nearly all her school reviews said vague things like, 'Elizabeth has made reasonable progress this term.' As she was sure that most of the teachers didn't know who she was, they couldn't really put anything else. 'Lacks confidence,' they sometimes said. Well, what did they expect her to do about that? Wouldn't *they* lack confidence if they kept being uprooted and made to go somewhere else?

This Elizabeth of the reviews, the Elizabeth who made reasonable progress but lacked confidence, was someone Tizzie hardly recognised as herself. She was someone the schools had made. The *real* Tizzie was so good at keeping herself hidden that even Tizzie herself wasn't sure who she was.

Fitting in was easier this time, because she was in Robin's tutor group and had all the same lessons, so needn't worry about being in the wrong place. Robin and her friend Jess took charge of her, introducing her to the teacher each time. Robin was the sort of person who did things without fuss, though there was a certain amount of 'Tizzie! Tizzie! Don't fly into a tizzy!' from other girls in the form. By the end of the day Tizzie had a locker of her own, a collection of new exercise books, and some Maths and French homework. It hadn't been too bad. She'd even been able to send a text message to Kamila, and Kamila had sent one straight back, saying *Miss u lots.*

The bus made its way home through the villages, gradually emptying. Tizzie and the boys got off at the Black Lion; Robin, who would stay on the nearly-empty bus as far as Upper Sleet, waved, and called, 'See you tomorrow!' And she'd asked Tizzie round for tea on Wednesday. It was just as well, though, that Robin already had Jess for a friend, because otherwise Tizzie would have felt disloyal to Greta. No one was going to get in the way of that friendship.

Tim Dingleby had stayed on at school for cricket, so it was just Lee who walked down the hill with Davy and Tizzie, as far as the stile. 'See you later,' he shouted, when they reached it. He broke into a run, kicking a stone ahead of him. When Tizzie was climbing the wobbly stile, he turned round to yell, 'Hey, Tizzie-Whizzy! Watch out for that creepy old man!' then ran on.

'What creepy old man?' Tizzie asked, pausing on the other side.

Davy made a rude gesture at Lee's back. 'Don't take any notice. He's just stupid.'

'But *which* old man? Did he mean Jack Doughty?'

'No,' said Davy. 'He meant Finnigan.' He turned from the road and vaulted over the stile, like a cross-country runner.

'But Finnigan isn't all that old,'Tizzy said, indignant. 'And he's not creepy. Why would anyone think he is?'

Davy shrugged, brushing past her along the narrow path. 'It's just – some people like to make up rumours. Stupid rumours. You know how Finnigan spends all his time at Roven Mere, and hardly leaves the place.'

Tizzie didn't. *'What* rumours?'

'I'm not telling you. It's rubbish, anyway. You'll go and tell your mum, and then she'll get scared and take you away.' Davy grinned. 'And I don't want your mum to leave, cos she's the best cook we've ever had. By miles.'

13
The Pony Paddock

Mum had made chocolate brownies, her speciality. Davy ate four, and Tizzy two. She thought about doing her homework, but decided it could wait till later. The afternoon was warm, the sun shining; it was too good to sit indoors learning French verbs.

'Change out of that uniform, Tizz, before you start doing anything messy,' Mum said, when Tizzie got up to follow Davy out of the kitchen.

She thought she might go down and see what Finnigan was doing, but Davy said, outside, 'I'm going to bring Ditty in. Come if you want.'

'Ditty? Who's Ditty?'

'Greta's pony. Haven't you seen her? She's in the paddock behind your cottage. Finnigan gives me pocket-money for looking after her. She stays out in the field now it's summer, but I fetch her up to the stable most days, to groom her and give her some feed.'

The paddock was at the far end of the orchard, and on lower ground, which was why Tizzie hadn't seen the pony from her window. There she was, grazing by the bottom fence, knee-deep in buttercups. Just as Tizzie knew she'd be, she was dapple-grey, with a pure white mane and tail. Tizzie hadn't met a pony before, and knew nothing about them, but this was the prettiest she'd ever seen.

'She's the pony in the picture, isn't she? Has Greta had her a long time?'

'What picture?'

'The one in Greta's bedroom. I mean in Greta's bedroom in the dolls' house,' Tizzie corrected herself, blushing. 'I saw it yesterday.'

'No, I don't think she can be. She's only been here a month. Finnigan bought her for when Greta comes home. There wasn't a pony here before. We've got three stables though. There used to be more, only they've been turned into garages.'

The pony had stopped grazing to look up at them. She made a small whickering sound, but didn't move. They made their way towards her, Davy swinging the rope halter. Brown butterflies, disturbed, rose from the long grass.

'So—' Tizzie couldn't work this out. 'Finnigan went and bought a pony to match the one in the picture? But how? You said he hardly leaves the place.'

'I don't know!' Davy said, laughing. 'P'raps he ordered one. Bought it on the internet and had it delivered.'

'Finnigan uses the internet?'

'Course he does. In the office. But p'raps for a pony he sent someone else to choose one.'

'So maybe Greta hasn't ever *had* a pony of her own?' Tizzie said, thinking aloud. 'Maybe this is the sort of pony she always wanted. Maybe she had the rocking-horse first, but wanted a real pony.'

'Don't ask me! Ask Finnigan. Lord Rupert must have told him to get it.'

'And paid for it?'

'Well, course,' Davy told her. 'Finnigan uses Lord Rupert's bank account for everything he buys. He wouldn't have spent his own money on a pony. They cost loads. 'Specially good ones, like this.'

'Do you know about ponies, then?'

'A bit,' said Davy. 'My mum taught me to ride when I was little. We lived on a farm where they kept horses. I ride Ditty sometimes—'

'It's a funny name!'

'Is it? It's short for something, I forget what. Finnigan wants her kept exercised, ready.'

'Ready for Greta.' Everything here, Tizzie thought, was for Greta. Did Greta *know*?

The pony stood still while Davy fastened the rope halter around her head. Her eyes were big, the darkest brown, with white lashes. Her curved ears pricked alertly. To Tizzie she was a creature of wonder, as strange as a unicorn. Reaching out a tentative hand, she touched the pony's neck, and the thick hair of her mane.

'She won't bite or anything,' Davy told her.

'Are you going to ride now?'

'No. But you can sit on her if you like, while I lead her up to the stable. She won't mind.'

'Can I?' Tizzie said eagerly. But how would she get on? With no saddle, there was nothing to get hold of; she was sure she couldn't jump up.

'Here,' said Davy. 'Bend your knee – no, your left one. Hold on to her mane, and when I say jump, you jump.'

With a hoist from Davy, Tizzie wriggled and scrambled herself astride. She hitched up her school skirt, feeling the pony's coat sun-warmed and smooth against her bare legs, slightly itchy.

'Hold on tight,' Davy said. He made a clicking sound with his tongue, and the pony walked forward.

How alive and alert and unpredictable she felt! At first Tizzy feared sliding right off, but found that she could sway to the movement, keeping in balance.

Davy led the pony through the gate to the orchard, and along the fence that ran all the way up to Cloud Cottage. Beginning to

98

enjoy herself, Tizzie thought: *I'm like Greta! Riding Greta's pony.* Except that Greta would no doubt be able to ride properly. Tizzie pictured her in smart jodhpurs and a helmet and shiny black boots, flicking a whip in the bossy way of riders. Greta was so lucky: she had everything she could possibly want, and more. For the first time Tizzie felt a prickling of resentment. What if Greta wasn't the generous friend she had imagined, the nice and funny companion? What if Davy was right when he called her a spoilt little cow? How could Greta *not* be spoilt, when she had a father who obviously doted on her?

With a jolt of surprise, Tizzie saw that someone was watching.

Mum. Standing by the fence of the Cloud Cottage garden, so still that Tizzie hadn't noticed her.

'Tizzie! What are you *doing?'* Mum shouted.

'Just riding!' Tizzie called back. Did it need explaining?

They drew level with Mum, and Davy brought the pony to a halt. Ditty lifted her nose over the fence, in a friendly manner; Mum stepped back.

'Tizzie, get off,' Mum said, her voice tight. 'Get off now.'

'But why?'

'Because I said so. Get down.'

Tizzie gave a theatrical sigh. *Why* did Mum have to do this – make her look about three years old, in front of Davy? She swung her right leg over the pony's neck and slithered to the ground.

'What's the problem?' She put on her stroppiest voice. 'What's wrong with me sitting on a pony for five minutes?'

'You're – you're not wearing a hard hat,' said Mum. 'It could be dangerous, riding ponies. It might bolt, rear, throw you off – you never know *what* it might do.'

'But you can see how quiet she is!' Tizzie retorted. 'And she's not an *it*, she's a *she*. Her name's Ditty, and she belongs to Greta, and Davy looks after her.'

'Oh, do you?' Mum looked directly at Davy for the first time. 'Well, you should have asked my permission before putting Tizzie on a pony. Go indoors, Tizzie. I want to talk to you.'

'For God's sake!' Tizzie retorted, but Mum's look told her not to argue any more. 'I'll see you later, Davy,' she mumbled, giving in.

Davy, with a bewildered shrug, led Ditty on past the cottage; Mum turned her back on Tizzie, and marched indoors.

'Mu-um! What was all that about?' Tizzie said, in the kitchen. 'Davy was only—'

'I don't want you getting involved with Finnigan and his daft ideas. *He* bought that pony – Mrs Crump told me. It's mad—'

'Mad, why?'

Mum busied herself with clearing up the dishes in the sink, left since breakfast. 'I told you. He's a bit – well, peculiar.'

'What, you mean dangerous?' Tizzie recalled what

Davy had said about rumours. 'But he isn't. Davy doesn't think so.' She thought of Finnigan telling her the story. 'He's nice, really.'

'I didn't say dangerous. I said peculiar.' Mum was scrubbing hard at a mug that surely didn't need such rigorous cleaning. 'And you could have changed your clothes, first. You've got your uniform all covered in horse-hair.'

'So why did you take the job, then, if you don't like him?'

'I didn't say I don't like him,' Mum said, sulkily.

'Oh, you're so mean!' Tizzie flared. 'It's *you* that's peculiar, if you ask me! You never tell me things, and you don't want me to have fun. How can I make friends, if I'm not allowed to do anything? What do you expect me to do – sit indoors all day?'

Mum turned on her. 'I expect you to do as you're told.'

'Yeah, well, sometimes I do and sometimes I don't. You'll just have to lump it. You don't *own* me!'

'While you live with me, I'm in charge of you. You do what I say.' When Mum was cross, her eyes were like drills, probing Tizzie's thoughts. Tizzie looked away.

'Haven't got much choice, have I? I have to do whatever *you* want. Go where *you* want. Live where *you* decide. I didn't want to come here, in the middle of nowhere! There's no one for me to be friends with, and even when there is, you have to interfere and spoil it. Davy must think I'm a complete wimp!

Not allowed to sit on a pony in case I fall off! Why are you so unfair? Why are you so mean all the time?'

The outburst had brought hot tears to her eyes. She blinked them back, furious. Through the blur she saw Mum looking at her, calmer now, but puzzled.

'But I thought you liked it here. With the house and the garden and everything. And you said school wasn't too bad.'

'Well, I *don't* like it! That's how much you know! I'd much rather live with Nannina. She's got room, hasn't she?

Mum made a sound like a pony snorting. 'Nannina? You're joking. She'd never agree to that. Nannina does exactly what she feels like doing. She'd hate to be lumbered with looking after someone else.'

'You *would* say that!' Tizzie hurled back. 'Lumbered! It's *me* that's lumbered. I'm going up to change.'

She flounced out of the room. When she came down again, in jeans and T-shirt, she left the cottage by the front door, without speaking to her mother.

14
The Dove-Grey Tourer

Tizzie had planned to go and find Davy in the stable, but tears still prickled her eyelids and she thought she might cry if she spoke to anyone. She didn't want Davy to see her crying, on top of everything, so she turned into the gardens and walked along by the lily-pond.

Almost at once, her bad mood began to evaporate. It was hard to feel grumpy, here by the fountain, with the water plashing gently and the sun warm on her face and arms. Two pinky-grey doves fluttered up to the roof of the well-house. Otherwise it was perfectly still. The scent of honeysuckle came to her in a drift.

Had she really told Mum that she didn't like it here? She hadn't meant that. Already, she felt in an odd way that she belonged here – that she'd come home to live, to stay. The place seemed to accept her, to know who she was.

She found herself remembering Finnigan's story about Peregrine, and his search for happiness. *Love is usually selfish,* he had said; at least that's what Peregrine thought. She wanted to know what Finnigan meant by that, and might have asked him, if it wasn't such a difficult question to come out with.

Was it true? If you thought you loved another person, was it only to get something for yourself?

Tizzie sat on a bench to think about it.

Once, at Nannina's, she and Mum had had one of their full-scale shouting matches. Tizzie ought to know that she could never win – however awful the things she said, she hurt herself more than she hurt Mum. It was Nannina who had come outside to find Tizzie in a crying temper, kicking a fence-post in the playground behind the block of flats. When Nannina asked what the matter was, Tizzie burst out, 'It's Mum! She hates me and I hate her!'

Nannina had been very upset by that. She sat Tizzie on one of the swings, and sat down herself on the next one. 'Your mum loves you very much,' she said. 'You're the most precious thing in her life. She loves you more than anything in the world.'

'She doesn't act like it!' Tizzie retorted.

'We don't, always. We're good at hurting the people

104

we care about most. But never, ever, even for a second, not even when she's very cross with you, does your mum stop loving you.'

Tizzie opened her mouth to argue, then fell silent, because deep inside she knew that it was true.

'And neither do I. It's just that we're not good at showing it,' Nannina said. In a waft of musky perfume, she leaned over to give Tizzie a hug. By *we* she seemed to mean herself and Mum. Maybe she'd passed on prickliness to Mum, the way Michael Rafferty had passed on his carroty hair to Tizzie. Nannina was a better cuddler than Mum, but neither of them was much good. Mum only hugged quickly and awkwardly, as if she didn't quite know the trick, and was embarrassed at catching herself trying. She wasn't like Kamila's mother, who was always kissing and cuddling Kamila and her brothers. But Tizzie wasn't sure anyway that she wanted quite as much petting as *that*.

Did Tizzie love Mum? As far as she knew what it meant, she supposed she did. They knew each other, the good and the bad. Mum could be unreasonable, irritable, spiky, *maddening* – but in their way of getting along as best they could, which often wasn't very well, they only had each other. So maybe that was what Finnigan (or Peregrine) meant by selfish: if the only reason for loving someone was the fear of having no one at all. Nannina was the only other person they could call Family, and now that they were so far from London, Tizzie wasn't sure when or how she'd see

Nannina again, unless she went to stay at half-term. Whatever Mum said, Nannina *did* like having her to stay – for a short time, anyway. Nannina often took Tizzie to the theatre or the cinema; once they'd even gone to a ballet. Maybe in the summer holidays – but there was no point planning as far ahead as that, because they probably wouldn't be here by then: Mum would abruptly decide she'd had enough, and would find a new job somewhere else, with or without a flat attached. Everything would go back in the boxes and into the van, and off they'd go.

Tizzie hated the thought of that: hated it with a fierceness that surprised her.

She got up from the bench, but instead of heading for the courtyard and the stables she took the track towards the workshop. She expected Finnigan to be doing something in there, but as she approached, she saw that he was cleaning out his caravan. A rug had been draped over the fence, and a bristly doormat, and the padded cushion from the bench. Finnigan was kneeling in the doorway with his front half inside the caravan and his back half out of it, watched by the cat, Small, who perched on the roof, watching intently.

'Hello,' Tizzie said politely.

Finnigan turned round, dustpan in one hand, brush in the other. 'Good afternoon, Tizzie. How was your day at school?'

'It was fine, thank you.' She looked past him, into the caravan. 'It looks very nice in there.'

'Do you like it? It's a 1950 Dove-Grey Tourer. Older than I am, and look at it! As good as the day it was made.' He got to his feet, brushing dust from the knees of his trousers. 'You're very welcome to take a look. No need to go in. You can see all there is to see from here.'

Tizzie looked. Although not quite like Dr Who's Tardis, the Dove-Grey Tourer seemed bigger inside than she'd have thought. There was a folding table, with the bench alongside. There was a little cooker, and two cupboards, and hooks for mugs and saucepans. There was a bed, covered with a patchwork quilt; there was even a little sink. At the end by the bed was a wide bay-window, curtained in a cheerful daisy fabric; on the shelf sat a radio, a vase of wild flowers, and some pieces of pottery.

'Oh, it's lovely!' Tizzie said.

Finnigan smiled. 'It's little, but quite big enough for me and Small. We've got everything we need.'

'We went on a caravan holiday, once, at Margate,' Tizzie told him. 'Mum and me, and my nan. The caravan was better than any flat we've ever lived in, but it wasn't as nice as this. It was bigger, and modern. Yours is special. Wouldn't you like to have wheels on it, and tow it around to different places?'

'It's a nice thought, but I don't want to be anywhere but here. Besides, I haven't got a car. Your nan, you said?' Finnigan had finished brushing the floor; he fetched the doormat, and put it back in position.

'Yes. Nannina. Mum's mum. She paid for Mum and me to go on the holiday, because Mum couldn't afford it.'

'I hope you enjoyed it,' Finnigan said, very seriously.

'Oh yes, we did, thanks.' She liked his way of talking to her as if she was a grown-up person, not someone to be bossed around or made to feel small.

'And have you got a grandad?' he asked.

'No. He died before I was born. There's just me and Mum and Nannina.'

They went over to the workshop. Finnigan called to Small, who made a chirruping sound in reply and jumped down from the caravan roof. Finnigan was making a grandfather clock for the dolls' house, a scaled-down version of the real one he'd repaired. Going to the bench, Tizzie looked at the puppet whose face she'd messed up yesterday.

'I think I'll have another go,' she said to Finnigan. 'It might turn out better this time.'

Finnigan smiled. 'Things often do.'

Tizzie began mixing paints, while Small settled near her on the bench, to watch.

This time, because she'd just been thinking about her nan, Nannina's face was clear in her mind, and the puppet's face turned out much better. A crinkly smile. Elegant arched eyebrows, like the ones Nannina drew on with a special pencil. Dark red lips, the colour of the lipstick Nannina always wore when she went out.

Ask Finnigan. Ask Finnigan. That was what she was always telling herself, when puzzles about Greta came into her mind. But now that she was here, and Finnigan was working silently, and there was no one to interrupt, and there could hardly be a better time, she simply couldn't come out with a direct question. The words formed themselves in her head, but she couldn't get them out through her mouth. The nearest she could get – and she had to leave her painting to look at the dolls' house, and the figures in the dining-room, to give herself an excuse – was to say, very hesitantly: 'This is Lord Rupert's wife, isn't it? What's her name?'

'Angel,' Finnigan answered, after a moment's pause.

'Angel?'

'Yes. Angel. Angeline. Angel is what Lord Rupert calls her.'

'Is she *Lady* Angel, then?'

'Her proper title is Lady Angeline Evershall,' said Finnigan. He was concentrating on cutting a strip of wood, pressing hard with a knife-blade.

'Don't you like her?' she asked; there was something in his voice.

'Tizzie!' He gave her a stern look over the top of his glasses; she had gone too far. 'How's that puppet coming on?'

Tizzie hung it on a hook, so that she could stand back to assess her progress. It had turned out better than she thought. She could almost smell Nannina's face-powder, and the sweet musk of her perfume.

'Very good!' said Finnigan.

'It's meant to be Nannina,' Tizzie told him.

Finnigan nodded. 'What clothes should she wear? We'll need to get them right.'

'She likes sort of dark, floaty, drapey clothes. Or things made of velvet. Mum calls her an old hippie. She wears dangly earrings and headbands and scarves and lots of bracelets. And she's got long hair, silvery-white. She does it in all sorts of knots and plaits and bunches, held up with spiky things and combs. Nannina was the one who first called me Tizzie, when I was a baby, and it stuck.'

'And what does she do, your Nannina?'

Tizzie thought. 'Well, she's got a part-time job at the cinema, selling tickets. She's got lots of friends, and two big dogs. She takes them for walks in the park. Even if it's pouring with rain, she still goes. She wears a bright yellow mack and wellies and a squashy hat.'

'I can almost see her.' Finnigan sounded wistful. 'Let's see what fabrics I can find.' He started rummaging in the box on the floor. 'You know, you could invite her here to visit you.'

The thought of inviting anyone here had never entered Tizzie's head. '*Could* we?'

'Of course! You and Morag must think of this as your home.'

'But—' Tizzie looked at him, wondering whether

to explain that *no*where was ever Home, not really. Instead, she asked, 'Have *you* got any family?'

'No. No one.' Finnigan picked up the cat and held it close; immediately it started purring, like a small engine. 'There's just me and Small,' he said, stroking the black fur. 'The two of us.'

15
The Wrought-Iron Gates

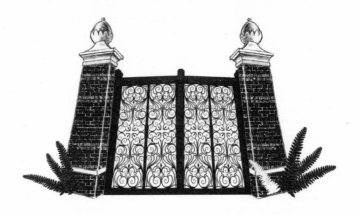

When Tizzie went to Robin's house after school next day, Robin's mum, Debbie, was out in the garden, with a toddling boy and a dog.

'That's Jay, and Jasper,' Robin told Tizzie, who wasn't at first sure which was which. It turned out that Jay was the little brother; he was just learning to walk, so Robin was on constant alert to stop him from straying too near the pond.

Debbie fetched choc-ices from the freezer, and they all sat eating them under the shade of an apple-tree.

'How are you settling in at Roven Mere?' Debbie asked. 'It must be a big change, after living in London.'

She was a comfortable sort of mum, a bit older than Tizzie's, and much more relaxing to be with.

'I love it,' said Tizzie. 'It's just so − so amazing.' She searched her mind for adequate words to describe her new home; failed, and asked instead, 'Have you been there?'

'No, never,' said Debbie. 'Only had glimpses through the gates. I wish they'd let people in, just once or twice a year − that's what it used to be like in the old days. They used to have a summer fair then, with boating on the lake and roundabout horses and a roast pig, and everyone from the village was invited.'

'The old days?' said Tizzie. '*How* old?'

'Oh, back in the time of the first Lord Rupert.' Debbie reached out a hand to stop the little boy from blundering into her chair.

'That was before I was born, wasn't it?' Robin said.

'That's right, love − before Dad and I came to live here. Your gran remembers him, though.'

Tizzie was puzzled. 'The *first* Lord Rupert? I didn't know there was another one.'

'He must have been this Lord Rupert's father,' Robin told her.

'No, I don't think he was,' said Debbie. 'I don't think the first one had a son − someone told me this one's his nephew. He must have inherited the title when the old Lord Rupert died. Gran would know.' She added to Tizzie, 'That's Robin's gran, my husband's mother. She lived here in the village long before we did.'

'And she said it had a different name, before.' Robin retrieved a piece of chocolate that had dropped on to her front, ate it, then dabbed at the smear it had left on her shirt. 'It wasn't called Roven Mere, back then.'

'That's right,' said Debbie. 'It used to be Paradise Hall, but the new Lord Rupert changed it to Roven Mere. I've always wondered why – Paradise Hall sounds like such a lovely place to live. Why would anyone change it?'

'Perhaps he didn't think it was Paradise? Perhaps he wasn't happy there?' Tizzie said, wondering aloud. 'But how could he know that, before he'd actually lived there? And surely he must have been happy.' She almost went on, 'I mean, he *looks* happy,' before remembering that all she'd seen was the painted figure in the dolls' house.

'Roven Mere's such a weird name,' said Robin. 'It sounds like it ought to be *Raven*.'

'I thought that at first,' Tizzie told her, 'but Roven Mere's the name of the lake, isn't it? He must have wanted to name the house after the lake.'

Debbie had smoothed out the wrapper of her choc-ice, and was folding and re-folding it. 'No – no, I don't think it was always called that. The lake was called Long Water. Robin's gran told me that. People used to go skating on it in winter when she was a girl.'

'All this name-changing!' Tizzie said. 'No wonder things are confused.'

'That manager chap might tell you,' Debbie suggested, 'if you can get any sense out of him. Mr

114

Finnigan, isn't it? He's a strange one, I've heard. Lives like a hermit. Hardly speaks to anyone. Hasn't left Roven Mere for years, so Jane Dingleby told me.'

'That's Lee and Tim's Mum,' Robin told Tizzie. 'She works there.'

Tizzie felt compelled to stand up for Finnigan. 'I like him, though. He's really nice. And he *does* speak. He speaks a lot. He tells me stories.'

'Really? Well, he must have taken a shine to you. No one else can get more than a word out of him, that's what Jane says.'

Tizzie wished she hadn't exaggerated; Finnigan had only told her one story, and in any case she should have kept it to herself, not come out with it as if it were somehow to her credit. But Robin's mum was talking about names again. 'It's Paradise Hall on all the old maps,' she was saying. 'It seems wrong to change the name of a house – unlucky. I mean, this is Forge Cottage, and there hasn't been a forge here for years and years, but we've kept the name because that's what it's always been. Gran says she remembers seeing the name Paradise Hall on those big gates.'

'Where it says Private, now,' Robin added. 'Perhaps too many people wanted to go in, if they thought it was the way to Paradise. Lord Rupert wanted to put them off, I bet. Keep it for himself.'

It still wasn't dark when Mum came to fetch Tizzie home. 'Morag, come in and have a drink!' Debbie urged her, but Mum, almost rudely, said that she needed to get back.

'You could have been friendlier!' Tizzie reproached, as they drove back along the lanes. The last blaze of the setting sun was low on the horizon, the sky streaked pink and charcoal-grey. 'What are you in such a hurry for, anyway? Debbie knows all sorts of interesting things. There used to be another Lord Rupert before our one, she says, and Roven Mere used to have a different name. I should have asked her about Greta, because Robin's gran knows all about—'

'I haven't got time for gossip,' Mum said. 'People out in the sticks are bound to wonder about a big place like Roven Mere. They haven't got much excitement in their lives.'

'Finnigan said we could invite Nannina here,' Tizzie remembered. 'That would be fun, wouldn't it?'

Mum gave a humourless laugh. 'Nannina? Are you joking? She's a London person. Can you see her out here, in the back of beyond?'

'But – doesn't she want to see where we're living? Not just to come for a day?'

'Nannina's got her own life,' Mum said. 'She wouldn't want any of this.'

Her shut-off expression warned Tizzie not to say any more. They were both silent for the last half-mile. Mum pulled up by the wrought-iron gates without saying anything; Tizzie jumped down, and pushed the gates open, their creak and whine sounding very loud in the still evening.

This was once the way to Paradise Hall, she thought. What would the name make you expect? Something

white and light, with spindly towers and turrets, and
pennants flying: a fairy-tale palace, maybe. But, as she
climbed back in, and saw Roven Mere stark and
severe against its background of trees, no light from
its windows and its tallest chimneys black against the
darkening sky, she knew that Roven Mere suited
it better.

16
The Dripping Trees

Lee Dingleby was a bit of a pain, Tizzie had decided from day one. He kept shouting out things like, 'Are you busy, Tizzie?' and, once, grabbed her rucksack and whirled her round in a circle, just so that he could taunt, 'Feeling dizzy, Tizzie?' He and his friends – including, to Tizzie's annoyance, Davy – seemed never to tire of this, finding it hilarious.

Robin only looked down her nose at them. 'I expect they'll grow out of it.'

On Thursday afternoon Tizzie got off the bus at the Red Lion, waving goodbye to Robin through the rain-streaked windows. Davy had left school early for a dentist appointment, so Tizzie set off alone down the hill. It had been raining in fits and spurts all day, but now the sky had darkened, threatening a real downpour.

'Oi! Tizzie-Whizzy!' someone yelled from behind.

It was Lee Dingleby, of course. He'd gone into the village shop, but was now walking very fast, half-running, gaining on her. At first she pretended not to hear, heading for the shelter of the trees by the bend in the road, but when he shouted again she turned and called back, 'What?'

'Wait a minute! I've got something to tell you!'

Tizzie reached the wobbly stile and climbed over. Lee skittered down the road, his feet slapping wetly; the side of the lane was ribboned with water, carrying leaves and soil with it. Tizzie pulled up the hood of her coat, and curled her hands inside the sleeves.

'This better be good,' she said crossly.

'Just thought you ought to know. I heard you on the bus, talking to Robin. You know, about Lord Whatsit and that weirdo, that old Finnigan.'

'Finnigan's not weird!'

'That's all you know. My mum does cleaning down at Roven Mere. She's known him longer than you have. And I've been down there with Davy, and seen him as well. I'm telling you, he's well weird. Creepy.'

'Is that what you've run after me for? I'm going home. Bye.' The rain was coming down harder now; Tizzie moved away from the stile, towards the trunk of the nearest tree.

'No, listen! I haven't started yet.'

'Started what?'

Lee climbed over the stile, almost tripping on the wonky cross-bar. 'He's told you about Lord Rupert, hasn't he, and Greta, and how they're coming back?'

'What if he has?'

'They're not,' Lee told her, grinning.

'What do you mean?'

'They're not coming back. It's all a big lie.'

'That's rubbish!' Tizzie turned away again. 'I'm not listening!'

Lee grabbed her arm. 'No, wait. How come Finnigan's the only one who ever hears anything from Lord Rupert – or says he does? How come no one else has even set eyes on Lord Rupert, or his wife or his daughter?'

'You're mad. You must be,' Tizzie told him. In fact he was beginning to look a bit frightening, with his hair plastered wetly to his head, and his eyes staring. 'You wouldn't talk like this if Davy was here. Davy's dad works for Lord Rupert, doesn't he? So does my mum. So does *your* mum – you've just said so. Who pays their wages, then, if there's no Lord Rupert?'

'Durr. Finnigan! Finnigan does.'

'Oh, right. Finnigan, who's so poor that he lives in a little caravan. He pays everyone's wages, does he? Don't be daft. Lord Rupert pays for everything. Davy told me.'

'Mum gets her money every Friday, that's right,' said Lee. 'Mrs Crump gives her a cheque, signed by

Finnigan. And the bank account's called *Roven Mere Estate.* Nothing about Lord Rupert.'

'So what does that prove?'

'I think,' Lee said, 'Lord Rupert and his family never went away.'

Tizzie took this in. All around and above her was the steady dripping of rain through the trees, mesmeric and oddly comforting.

'But you said—'

'They never went away,' Lee repeated. 'What everyone said was, they went away, and Finnigan came. But I don't think they *did* go. I think—' He paused for effect. 'I bet he killed them.'

'Oh, now you're just being horrible!'

'Killed them,' Lee repeated. 'Murdered them for their money. And ever since then, to cover up, he keeps saying they'll be back soon, they're on their way. And he pretends to keep everything ready.'

'He doesn't pretend. Everything *is* ready.' Tizzie turned to go. 'I'm not even listening, if you're going to talk such garbage.' But the rain was coming down hard enough now to make her linger, reluctant to leave the shelter of the tree.

'Up to you,' Lee said. 'But think about it! You've got to admit, it's a weird set-up down there. Finnigan's conned you, just like he's conned Davy.'

'That's all you know,' she retorted. 'Finnigan's hardly told me anything at all. What about your mum, then? Why does she work there, if she thinks Finnigan's a murderer?'

'I didn't say *she* thinks that. She thinks there's something funny going on, but the pay's better than she'd get anywhere else, so she stays.'

'Right. So it's only *your* stupid idea, the murder.'

'Not just mine,' Lee said obstinately. 'Me, and Tom Jenkins, and Andy Smith – we've worked it all out.'

'So I suppose you've worked out what Finnigan did with the bodies?'

'There's a well, isn't there? And a lake. Easy enough for him to get rid of them.'

Tizzie was beginning to shiver. Dampness was leaking into her shoes; she felt cold and clammy inside her raincoat. Lee's words were ganging up on her, demanding to be listened to. They grouped themselves into headlines and stories: HORRIFIC MURDER AT COUNTRY MANSION. BODIES FOUND IN WELL. They trumpeted themselves in her brain; they made her feel small and helpless and afraid. But she wasn't going to let Lee see that.

'Yeah, right,' she said, loading her voice with scorn. 'You'll be telling me the place is haunted, next. You don't scare me with your pathetic story. I'm going home now.'

'OK! Just thought you ought to know. Don't get in a tizzy.'

'Why don't you *grow up!*' she flung at him, and marched off through the trees as fast as she could, with the path turned to slippery mud under her shoes. She turned round once to make sure he wasn't following, walked as far as the lower edge of the copse, then hesitated again, seeing the rain sweeping across the rough meadow below. She'd better wait under the trees till it eased off.

Waggling her arms to shake the raindrops off her sleeves, she stood dripping, and thinking. She looked down at the gravel driveway and the east front of Roven Mere, which now looked as grey and forbidding as it had on her first sighting.

She was thinking about Finnigan. How kind he was, how he listened to her, gave her things to do, and praised her. How he gave her his attention in that grown-up way. How he'd told her a story. How nice his face was, with the rimless glasses that magnified his eyes. How stern he could look, how rarely he smiled, and how his face lit up when he did. How tender his expression became when he held the cat in his arms.

Finnigan a murderer? No! It was just something Lee and his friends had made up, for a laugh. Finnigan, Tizzie realised, was the person she liked best at Roven Mere: better than Davy, better than Mrs Crump. Almost better than Mum, for whom her feeling was too complicated to be called *liking* at all.

She couldn't stand here indefinitely, and the rain showed no sign of easing up. Head down, she forged on through the wet grass of the meadow. It was mad, what Lee had said. Obviously it was, all of it. Mad or malicious. And he was going to look pretty stupid when Greta came home.

Soon. Please! *Soon.*

17

The Boat-House

For all her certainty, Tizzie was awake and worrying in the early hours of Saturday morning.

Did people really say such nasty things about Finnigan? People in the village, like Lee Dingleby's mother – people who worked here, and ought to be loyal? According to Lee, Finnigan was a liar – nothing he said could be trusted. And hadn't Mum said almost the same thing? *He's a strange man,* she had told Tizzie. *Peculiar. I don't want you listening to what he says.*

But Tizzie liked listening to Finnigan. She *did* believe him. And Davy did, too, didn't he? Besides,

Davy believed Greta was coming home; that was why he was looking after the pony, and helping with the dolls' house. And he'd said that Greta was a spoilt little cow. Tizzie didn't like that version of Greta, but she preferred it to the one that was lying murdered and eaten by fishes in the lake, or at the bottom of the well.

Tizzie got out of bed and opened her curtains.

It was cool today after the rain, hazy. The trees in the orchard seemed to beckon to her through pearly mist.

Moving quietly about the cottage, she got herself washed and dressed. What she most wanted to do was to go up to the big house; to carry on exploring the rooms, with no one to stop her. But the house would be locked up; of course it had to be, at night, with no one living in it. Mum had her own keys, and unlocked the kitchen door each morning when she went to start work; Mrs Crump had keys too, and so did Finnigan. Tizzie went to Mum's raincoat, hanging on the hook by the back door, and felt in the pockets, but the keys weren't there. That meant Mum must have them upstairs in the bedroom. It might be possible to creep in and look for them; but no, Mum would wake up and be cross. There would be time later to explore the house, with no need of keys.

So, instead, Tizzie let herself out of the cottage and walked down towards the lake.

The mist was thicker here, seeming to hold everything in hushed silence; even the birds seemed subdued. The farthest shore was blurred and grey; the trees on the small island appeared to be rootless, floating in vapour.

Half-way down the slope, Tizzie stopped walking. What was she doing here? Hadn't she had enough of a fright last time? And that was before Lee had put his stupid ideas into her head ...

A movement caught her eye, a dark shape. From the nearest shore, from the boat-house below her, the little rowing-boat was heading out into the lake. She saw its silvery wake, and a huddled figure plying the oars; she heard the dip and ripple.

Tizzie caught her breath before realising that it would be Jack Doughty, of course. Davy had told her that Jack Doughty liked to go fishing in the lake. She couldn't see Mac, his Labrador, but perhaps he didn't take the dog with him in the boat in case it barked and whuffed, and scared the fish away.

Instead of going down to the lake shore, she found a different path that ran along the slope and then looped back towards the main house, returning through a gate at the far end of the track that led past Finnigan's workshop and caravan. All was quiet there; the caravan curtains drawn, the workshop closed up. Tizzie walked on by, as far as the courtyard. Not wanting to go back indoors yet, she went down to the pony paddock. Ditty was standing by the gate; her ears pricked as she saw Tizzie coming, and she made her whickering sound of welcome. She must be lonely, Tizzie thought. Always waiting: like Roven Mere itself.

It was odd how time seemed to stretch itself out, so early in the day. Tizzie ran her fingers through the pony's tangled mane, and pictured herself and Greta coming out early like this. They'd have agreed the night before to meet at the stable or the paddock gate. They'd set off together, one riding, one walking, taking it in turns. Greta would teach Tizzie how to ride properly, and they'd go far from Roven Mere, along the valley, along the ridge of the hill, exploring together, telling each other secrets, giggling. Being best friends, the best and closest friends.

When she turned back towards Cloud Cottage, she saw that someone was watching her. It was him – Jack Doughty, standing under the arch of the courtyard, with Mac sitting alertly beside him. She gave a little wave, intending to go back up through the cottage garden, but Jack waved back and started walking towards her. With this permission, the dog bounded ahead.

Tizzie waited, accepted Mac's licky greeting, and wondered how Jack could have moored the boat and got back up here so quickly. He never seemed to move very fast, always at the same ponderous pace, while Mac covered six times the distance running back and forth. By now, she was used to Jack's presence at mealtimes, and his odd way of staring, with eyes that seemed filmed over. He was staring at her now, very hard: then he said, 'Did you see her, then?'

'See who?' Tizzie turned round, thinking he must mean the pony, who stood in full view by the gate.

'Greta! She was there.'

'*Where?*'

'On Long Water. Rowing her little boat.'

'But it can't have been her. I mean, I was there. I thought it was – I mean, you must have been mistaken. It's so misty—' Although, now that she looked around, the mist had almost cleared, a watery sun showing through.

'It was her,' said Jack Doughty. 'I swear it was.'

'What, is she still there? I'm going back to see!'

Tizzie set off at a run, up the slope to the stile, her heart pounding; her eyes scanned the lake as soon as it came into view. Only the faintest trails of mist now hung above the water. There was no boat in sight; no ripples disturbed the still surface, apart from the wake of a moorhen bobbing among the reeds. Greta must have rowed back to the boat-house – but maybe she was still there.

Tizzie ran down the rough path, turning crabwise for the descent; ricking her ankle with a yelp of pain, stumbling, righting herself, careering on. 'Greta!' she called, as soon as she was close enough to be heard. 'Greta!'

What would she say next? 'It's me! It's Tizzie! I've been waiting for you!' And Greta, the Greta of the portrait with her hair brushed and shining, would look at her in surprise and delight. They would walk back to the house, talking and talking. By the time they arrived, it would seem that they'd been friends for ever. 'Where've you been, you two?' people would say. Because no sooner would they meet than they'd be 'you two'. Tizzie and Greta. Greta and Tizzie. Inseparable.

'Greta?' she called again, one hand on the boat-house roof, as she rounded the bank and turned in at the open front.

Her voice seemed to bounce back emptily. The boat was moored there, just as she'd seen it the first time. The oars were neatly paired, lying over the bows.

Disappointment was a choking lump in her throat, a thud in her stomach. She had to blink and look again to convince herself that the boat-house really was empty. No Greta. No one at all. Nothing to show that the boat had ever been untied from its moorings.

But it *had*! She'd seen it – definitely seen it. So had Jack Doughty; she couldn't have been hallucinating.

Greta had been here. And that meant she must be somewhere around. At the house! Obviously that's where she'd go. The distance from lake to house seemed endless, as Tizzie puffed up the hill again, through the courtyard and along the track.

As the mansion came into view, she saw that a red post van had stopped outside the main door, and Mrs Crump was speaking to the driver, who handed over a bundle of letters and packets.

'Morning, Tizzie.' Mrs Crump, sorting through the envelopes, turned to go up the steps and indoors.

Tizzie ran after her. 'Wait! Is Greta here?'

'Greta? No, dear, no. What makes you think that?'

Tizzie explained that Jack Doughty had seen her on the lake; but Mrs Crump only shook her head and said, 'Well, I don't see how she'd get here all on her own. Finnigan didn't say they'd be here today.'

She was watching the postwoman, who reversed her van neatly before giving a little toot; Mrs Crump waved a hand. Tizzie glanced at the stack of post she was clutching. The letter on top was addressed to *Lord Rupert Evershall, Roven Mere, Sleet, Gloucestershire.*

'No, not today,' Mrs Crump continued, her attention back with Tizzie. 'Thursday week, he's expecting them, last I heard. Apparently he got a letter yesterday.'

Then, Tizzie thought, they must have come early. That was the only explanation. Wouldn't everyone need to know? Especially Mum, if she was expected to serve splendid meals in the dining-room? It would be up to Finnigan to tell everyone – but did *he* know?

On her way to the workshop – surely Finnigan would be up and about by now – she met Jack Doughty coming the other way with his dog, heading, she supposed, for his flat above the stables.

'Seems I was wrong just now,' he told her gruffly. 'It wasn't her. Wasn't Greta after all. Course it wasn't. My eyesight's not as good as it was.'

'Oh!' Tizzie was deflated. 'But then – who was it?'

'Dunno. One of them boys from the village, could've been, helping theirselves to her boat. We ought to put a stop to that.'

Tizzie trudged on, sagging with disappointment, tired from all the walking and running she'd done; and only now did she remember that she'd had no breakfast. What if Jack Doughty had made a mistake

– made a mistake about being wrong? She was unwilling to give up the idea that Greta might be close, so close. But then, taking the boat out seemed exactly the sort of thing Lee Dingleby might do. He'd be delighted if he knew how much confusion he'd caused.

Still, there was a letter from Lord Rupert! Mrs Crump had said so. And Thursday week wasn't too long a time to wait.

18
The Box Hedge

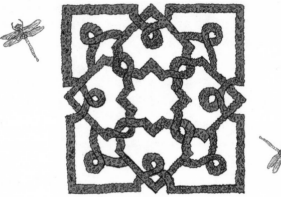

Davy and Finnigan were coming along from the workshop, Davy pushing a wheelbarrow, Finnigan carrying garden forks and spades. The barrow was loaded with small green plants, dozens of them.

'We're getting on with the Knot Garden today,' Finnigan told Tizzie. 'Come and help, if you like.'

'What's a Not-Garden?' Tizzie asked, imagining something paved in concrete.

'A garden that's got to be ready for Thursday week,' Davy told her.

Tizzie smiled. 'That's the day they're coming home, isn't it?'

'Who told you that?' Finnigan said sharply.

'Mrs Crump did. She said you had a letter from Lord Rupert.'

'Yes, so there's a lot to get ready. No time to lose,' said Finnigan. 'A Knot Garden, Tizzie, is a garden in a formal design. The knots are made by low box hedges, twining in a pattern, with other plants in between.'

'Box?' Tizzie pictured a hedge made of cardboard.

'Box is the name of a plant,' Finnigan said, nodding towards the shrubs clustered on the barrow. 'Dense and bushy, easily clipped into shape.'

If he'd been on his own, Tizzie would have told him about Jack Doughty thinking he'd seen Greta. Instead she glanced at Davy. Could it have been *Davy* who was out on the lake this morning? There was no real reason why it shouldn't be; he was allowed to ride Greta's pony, so why shouldn't he row her boat? She'd ask him later.

'We're moving the dolls' house today, as well,' Davy told her. 'Into Greta's room.'

In that case, Tizzie thought, she'd better get a good look at it first. There was something she wanted to check out. Both houses, the real one and the dolls' house, were oddly lopsided, with the tower or turret at one of the corners farthest from the entrance. In reality this faced into the trees; on the dolls' house, with no woodland behind, it looked more promi-nent. As there were small windows on several levels, there must be some way up inside it: a flight of stairs from the top corridor, perhaps. Davy probably knew, but Tizzie liked the idea of discovering it for herself. There was bound to be something interesting there, even if only the view from the highest windows in the house.

The wheelbarrow had to be lifted up various steps, and manoeuvred through narrow places, before they were in the garden-in-progress Tizzie had seen before. The patterns where the little hedges would go had been marked out with sprinkled chalk. Now, the box plants – dozens of them – were to be put in position. Davy's Dad, Will Crump, was already there, digging trenches.

'Won't there be flowers?' Tizzie asked, as the box was just plain green.

'Yes,' Will told her, 'in the spaces between. That'll be lavender. Then there'll be a climbing rose and a jasmine to go over the arch behind the seat. Be good for bees, this will. There's to be a special marble bench, as well, and a dovecot, with white doves. That's what Lord Rupert wants.'

'It'll look lovely,' Tizzie said politely. Cheered by the way everyone was talking about Lord Rupert in such a matter-of-fact way, she helped Will to arrange the box shrubs, placing them at intervals ready for Will to plant. But she didn't see why Finnigan was taking such a keen interest: checking measurements, replacing one shrub with another, standing back to assess the effect. Will Crump was the gardener, after all.

They worked all morning, till half the box shrubs were planted. A local nursery, Finnigan said, was to deliver all the other plants on Monday, and the marble bench was being specially made.

'But what's it all *for?*' Tizzie asked Davy, as they walked up to the house at lunch-time. 'Is the garden going to be open for visitors, or something?'

'Do you really need to ask? It's for Greta. Greta's Garden.'

Of course she should have known.

They trooped into the kitchen, Will behind them, Finnigan coming more slowly.

Will kicked off his gardening boots outside the door, then sniffed appreciatively as he entered. 'Mmm, something smells good! I'd toil all day for one of your meals, Morag!'

Tizzie's mum, carrying plates to the table, smiled back at him: a really nice smile, her prettiest. 'It's only bread and soup and salad.'

'Yes, but it's *your* bread and soup and salad.'

Hmm, Tizzie thought. He likes her. And she likes him. *That's* interesting.

But she noticed that Mum's smiles disappeared as soon as Finnigan came in. Mum would hardly look at him, let alone speak.

19
The Platter of Trout

'And it's for Greta, of course. Finnigan says it's got to be ready for Thursday week, because it's a special anniversary.' Tizzie had stayed in the kitchen to help Mum put things away; she felt so optimistic today that she couldn't help chatting. 'Of what, I wonder? He didn't say birthday. Perhaps it's a wedding annivesary – Lord Rupert's and Lady Angeline's? But then the garden would be for them, not for Greta—'

'*Please* will you stop going on about Greta?' Mum said, from the fridge. 'You've been talking about nothing else!'

'Who do you think it was, though, rowing on the lake?'

'How should I know? Could've been anyone, anyone at all.' Mum came to the table with a platter of fish, seven of them. They were strong and muscular, with silvery scales shimmering purple and green. Their big mouths gaped in disapproval; their flat eyes stared swimmily at the ceiling. Tizzie gazed at them. She liked fish to eat, but she wished they didn't have to lie there quite so obviously dead.

'Are they from the lake? Did Jack Doughty catch them?'

'No, Will got them for me. They're rainbow trout. I'm going to bake them for dinner.'

Will got them for me. Hmm, Tizzie thought. Clever Will. He must have known that Mum would be far more delighted with fresh trout to cook than with flowers or chocolates, if he'd wanted to give her a present.

'Still,' Tizzie said, her thoughts returning to the mysterious rower, 'it was a cheek, wasn't it, taking Greta's boat without permission?'

Mum threw up her hands. 'Greta's boat! Greta's pony! Greta's garden! You'd think no one else mattered!'

'But I was only—'

Tizzie expected Mum to flounce into the larder, but instead she sat down at the table. 'Tizzie,' she said quietly. 'Don't get your hopes up too high. You're going to be disappointed.'

'Disappointed?'

'Because – because all this talk of Thursday week, it's a build-up to nothing. No one's coming.'

Tizzie stared at her. 'But they are! What's everyone getting ready for, then? How would *you* know, anyway?'

'I just have a feeling,' Mum said obstinately.

'Well, so do *I* have a feeling! You don't know everything! Anyway,' Tizzie said in triumph, 'Finnigan's got a letter! A letter from Lord Rupert. Why don't you ask him to show you, if you don't believe him?'

There was a pause, then Mum said quietly, 'Why don't you?'

'What?'

'Ask him to show you that letter.'

'Right, I will. I'll go and ask him now.'

Mum fetched a sharp knife from the block, flipped one of the fish on to its side, pulled back the flap of its gills and started slicing.

Appalled, fascinated, Tizzie shrank back. 'Yeuch!'

'Don't be such a wimp!' Mum told her. 'You'll be keen enough to eat them, when they're baked with lemon and herbs. Weren't you going?'

Tizzie went. She looked first in the Knot Garden, but Will was there with Davy, still planting. No sign of Finnigan. He must have gone down to the workshop.

The doors were open now; Tizzie heard hammering from inside. Small sat in the entrance; he miaowed a remark, and twined himself around her legs, purring.

There at the workbench was Finnigan, bent over the dolls' house, tacking fabric to its complicated roofs. He looked up as she came in. 'Nearly ready. I've found some bits for your Nannina puppet. Look.'

He'd chosen printed Indian fabric, deep red velvet and purple silk, gauzy black, a ribbon studded with gemstones, a scrap of fake fur.

'That's brilliant – thank you! Just right for Nannina – how did you know?'

'You told me. Here's needles and pins and staples, if you want to have a go at dressing her.'

Tizzie didn't know where to start. It was lucky that Nannina liked loose drapey things, which might not need much sewing, or (more importantly) skill. She picked up the purple silk and tried draping it around the puppet – which now had hair! Long white hair. Nannina hair.

'It's from Perdita's tail,' Finnigan told her.

'Whose?'

'Perdita. The pony. Ditty, Davy calls her.'

'They're both nice names,' Tizzy said, 'but I think I like Perdita better. Did *you* give her that name?'

Finnigan nodded. 'Perdita is a girl in a play.'

'A play? So there's a story about her?' Tizzie said eagerly.

'Yes, there is.'

Tizzie was trying to thread a needle. 'Oh, can I hear it?'

'No, I don't think I want to tell you that one. But there's another, if you'd like it.'

'Please!'

Finnigan paused in his tacking for a moment, gazing out of the doorway as if collecting his thoughts. Then he began, 'It goes like this . . .

Once there was a man who wanted to know what happiness was—'

'But you told me that one!' Tizzie was disappointed. 'Peregrine, and the string of moments, like pearls.'

Finnigan looked at her gravely. 'That's right, I did. But this was a different man – because other people than Peregrine have asked themselves the same question. And it was another time, and another place.

This man who wanted to know what happiness was, his name was Thaddeus. Thaddeus had made himself a garden, and nothing gave him more pleasure than to walk around it in the evening, and see what he'd made.

It was the middle of winter, when the day is the shortest and the night the longest of the year. Thaddeus had made his garden to look beautiful in winter as well as in summer, for he knew that part of a garden's beauty is in its bones, in its skeletons best seen when there are no leaves to soften the outlines, when the sun casts long rays, and frost silvers the bare branches.

In the centre of his garden he had made a round pond, a perfect circle, bordered by grass. On this winter night, Thaddeus walked in his garden by the light of the moon. Which is of course the light of the sun, reflected palely from the moon's face. The moon was full, a perfect silver disc in the sky. And that's what Thaddeus saw, reflected in his round pond. The moon was so silver, so calm, so beautiful, that he wanted to keep it in his pond, where he could look at it whenever he chose. When he went indoors and got into bed, he was disconsolate. He saw the moon through his window and knew that by morning it would have sailed across the sky and into daylight, and would be no longer visible. And, worse, it would change, night by night – waxing and waning. Some nights it would not appear at all, when it hid behind clouds; sometimes it would peep through them in a coy and teasing manner.

He wanted the moon to be constant, always there for him to look at. Always reflected in his pond. He wanted it to be his, and his alone. He fell asleep, puzzling how to keep it.

While he was sleeping, the night grew colder and colder, and the pond froze over. In the morning Thaddeus rushed out to the garden and stood shivering in his dressing-gown and slippers. His pond was all covered over with thick ice and hoar frost. Anything inside it would be trapped under the ice.

'That's the answer,' he thought to himself. 'Instead of letting the moon sail on by each night, I must trap and keep it.'

Next night was milder, and the moon still full and round. Thaddeus dressed up warmly and waited by a tree, until the moon was overhead, reflected perfectly in his pond. He had put ready a big pile of branches and bracken, and a heap of soil, and a shovel. Quickly he got to work. He piled branches and bracken over the moon, till not a feature of its silver face could be seen. Then with his shovel he piled earth over the top.

'Now I have my Moon Pond,' he said to himself. 'With the moon captured in it, for ever. Mine, to keep.'

He went to bed content. Next morning he returned to pile more earth, and he stamped and stamped until he'd made a squidgy, muddy mound where once the pond had been. So never again did he see the moon reflected in his pond, but he knew that it was in there.

Thaddeus thought he should have been happy, but he wasn't.

There was a little fallow deer that came to his garden. So pretty was she, so slender and dappled, so graceful as she moved, so full and brown her eyes. But she came and she went, and some days she did not come at all. Thaddeus wanted to have her and keep her for himself. He thought of building a pen and keeping her in that, but soon he had a better idea.

'I will have her made in stone,' he said to himself.

So he found a skilful stone-carver, and described the deer to him.

'I must see the original,' said the stone-carver, 'for there are deer and there are deer, but this particular deer is the one you want.'

Thaddeus could see no answer but to shoot the deer dead, and take it to the stone-carver's workshop. So he lay in wait with his rifle, and shot the little creature through the heart as she came to drink from his stream.

How fine-boned her limbs were, how soft her dappled coat, how sharp her little hooves! How perfect she was, and how dead!

But he had her now. She was his. He carried her to the stone-mason, and the stone-mason made a copy. Thaddeus paid him handsomely, and then he returned home, carrying both deer with him, the stone one and the dead one. Then he dug a grave in the mound of earth, and there he buried the corpse of the fallow deer. The statue he placed nearby.

Now Thaddeus had his moon and his deer, but neither made him happy. The mound of earth dried out over the pond, and weeds grew in it. The statue of the deer was graceful enough, but it could not have her quick eyes, her dappled colour and fleeting movement. Thaddeus looked at his mound of dried mud and his piece of cold stone, and something in him craved for more. What it was he wanted, he didn't know. But the wanting was an ache deep inside him.

'Will I never be happy?' he moaned to himself.

He prowled around his garden again, asking himself that question, looking for answers.

Spring was coming now, and from the bushes there sang a voice of astonishing beauty. Full-throated and vibrant, it sang in the dusk. It sang of sadness and of joy. It sang of life and of hope. And, to Thaddeus, it sang of happiness.

While that bird was singing, he could think of nothing else. That incomparable voice filled his ears and his head and his heart. When he went to bed, he dreamed of that joyous sound.

'If only I had that voice, to hear whenever I wanted, I should be happy,' he told himself.

This time, he made a cage. He made the most beautiful cage imaginable, and he painted it gold. Then he set out to trap the bird. Knowing the bird's favourite singing-perch, he surrounded the bushes with nets. When the bird began to pour forth its song, he threw an even larger net over the thicket. The bird fluttered and thrashed and panicked, but it was caught.

When Thaddeus held it in his hand, he was surprised to see that it was just a plain brown bird. From its voice he had expected something golden like an oriole, or jewelled like a humming-bird. But he had it now, small and dull as it was.

He placed it in its cage, and carried it indoors, and waited. Every day he waited by the bird-cage for the brown bird to sing, and bring him joy.

The bird remained silent. Not a note did it utter. It would not eat nor drink. It sat sullenly on its perch. Sometimes it battered its wings against the bars of its cage until it fell exhausted to the floor.

It would surely die.

And soon it did. It lay lifeless and silent, its glorious voice extinguished.

Now Thaddeus was more miserable than ever. He buried the dead bird in the mound of mud. All his efforts had come to nothing! He was no more happy than before. He found no joy whatsoever in his mud-mound and his stone deer.

But he kept searching and searching for happiness. And still he searches to this day, no closer to finding it, and not a jot wiser.'

Finnigan stopped talking. His face was drawn; it seemed that telling the story had left him bleak and weary.

'Is that it?' said Tizzie, looking up from her puppet.

'Yes, it is.'

'Did you make it up?' she asked, though she guessed what he would say, and he did:

'You never really know with stories. It's hard to know where they come from.'

She couldn't help saying, 'I don't think it's such a good story as the other one. And you can't end there!'

'Why not?'

'You should have made things come right.'

'Does Thaddeus deserve that?'

'Maybe he doesn't,' Tizzie said, after a moment, 'but the deer and bird do. And the moon. Couldn't he have a chance to try again?'

Finnigan examined the dolls' house roof from all angles, giving a gentle tap here and there with his hammer. Then he looked at her keenly. 'Maybe you could do it! Make up a better ending for him.'

'Me? End the story?'

He nodded, and waited. Tizzie considered.

'Only if I'm allowed to go back a bit,' she said. 'Before the bird died. Listen, it could go like this:

Thaddeus watched the poor bird getting weaker and weaker in its cage. He knew that it would die soon if it went on like that. I mean, he was stupid, but not <u>that</u> stupid. So there was only one thing to do. He opened the door of the cage and watched the bird fly out. It flew right out of the window and into the garden. He hoped it would start singing, but it didn't. Instead it flew to the mound of earth and perched on top. It started pecking. It pecked and pecked and sent dirt flying everywhere. So Thaddeus went closer to see what it was pecking for. When he knelt down, he saw that something was trying to get out. A little nose, a—' she searched for the right word '—snout, pushing through the earth. It pushed and it pushed until the little deer sprang out, alive after all. She shook the dirt off her coat and started bounding round in circles.

Then Thaddeus looked into the muddy hole she'd

146

come out of, and even though it was daylight he thought he saw a little glimpse of the moon, still trapped in there. So he fetched his shovel and started digging, and pulling away the branches. He dug for so long that it got dark. At last he'd dug out as much as he could. There was only a little bit of muddy water in the bottom of the pond now, because it had got – you know – sucked up by the earth. And half-sunk in it was the moon, buried like a silver plate, only gone all dull with dirt and mud. Thaddeus reached in his hands and tried to pick it up, thinking he'd clean and polish it. But his hands couldn't get hold of it. Then he realised it wasn't really there at all, and he nearly cried. But he stood up, and he looked up at the sky, because that's where he should have been looking all the time. There was the moon, high above, with its silver face. And that made him <u>happy</u>. Because it was like the moon was his reward for doing a good thing, after all the stupid things he'd done. And then the bird started to sing, and that made him even happier.

'So!' she said. 'That's my ending. What do you think?'

'I think it's very good, Tizzie,' said Finnigan. 'You're right – it's much better than mine. You did well to give Thaddeus another chance. Lucky man.'

'Don't you know any *happy* stories?' she asked him.

'I do. I do indeed. But they must wait till their time comes. Did you enjoy that, finishing my story?'

'I did!' she said, surprised, because she always found it quite hard to write stories at school. 'I liked the way it just came out, without me exactly knowing what was going to happen. But all the same I knew that *something* would.'

'Good! You're a story-teller's daughter, after all,' Finnigan said. 'And now you're a story-teller yourself.' He looked over the top of his glasses at the puppet. 'Now, that really is starting to look like Nannina. Do you think?'

Tizzie had been cutting and shaping and sewing all this while. The puppet was now wearing a long skirt and a swathed top, and soon it would have a scarf and a hair-band. Tizzie knew how clumsy her stitches were, and how she'd got knots in her thread and jabs in her fingers. But she couldn't *see* that. All she could see was that the puppet was starting to look rather good.

Only now did she remember that she'd gone to the workshop to ask to see Lord Rupert's letter. But how could she? How could she come out with a question like that? Finnigan would think that she needed proof before she could believe what he said.

So she didn't ask.

20
The Knot Garden

In the evenings, after supper was eaten and cleared up, Mum usually stayed in the kitchen. She cleaned the oven, or she made lists and planned menus. She'd suddenly decide to bake a cake, or make tartlets, or mix bread dough to rise overnight. She almost lived in the kitchen, only going back to Cloud Cottage to sleep. On her day off, she went into Gloucester and came back with yet another recipe book and a set of measuring jugs. Tizzie couldn't understand how anyone could live at Roven Mere but take so little interest in the gardens and grounds. When Mum had a couple of hours off, she sat on the terrace with

Good Food magazine or her latest cookery book, but went no farther.

As soon as Tizzie asked Finnigan if she could use the computer in his office, explaining that she wanted to email her friend, he looked surprised. 'Yes, of course you can. Why haven't you asked before?'

So now Tizzie could email Kamila every day, and swap news. She sent messages to Nannina as well; but she knew that Nannina didn't like email, only checked her in-box on Sundays, and then sent the briefest of replies. 'Finnigan said you could come and visit,' Tizzie typed. 'Why don't you? It'd be fun to show you round.' But Nannina shrugged off the idea, just as Mum had said she would. 'Not my kind of place. Morag was mad to go there. You'll soon be back in London, if I know my daughter.'

Once, leaving the office, Tizzie met Mum coming down the back stairs that led from the ground floor. She seemed furtive, although there was no reason why she shouldn't be there. When Tizzie said, 'Where've you been?' Mum sidled past and said, 'Oh, just looking for Mrs Crump.'

Tizzie gave her a sideways look, which Mum chose to ignore. Mrs Crump had gone home to Mere Lodge, as they both knew, to watch something on TV.

There was a TV in Cloud Cottage, too, but Tizzie hardly watched it. Most evenings, she left her homework till after supper, then she and Davy both spread out their books on the table in the big kitchen. On the days when she and Mum were cross with each other, she worked instead on her bedroom floor. Really, though, she preferred the kitchen: the warm smell of baking, and she and Davy helping each other: he was good at Maths but struggled with French, Tizzie the reverse. Often Will stayed on after supper to talk to Mum over coffee or a beer; Mrs Crump drifted in and out with bits of chat and gossip. Finnigan always left straight after the meal, thanking Mum politely. Other than that, they hardly spoke to each other. It was obvious to Tizzie that Mum didn't like Finnigan nearly as much as she liked Will. Sometimes Tizzie saw Finnigan looking at Mum a little sadly, as if he couldn't work out why.

What if he sacked her, deciding to find a friendlier cook? What if Mum was just too rude?

Tizzie listened especially hard when Mum and Will were talking, but they never said anything particularly interesting. When the homework was finished, she would put her school books in her rucksack and go out into the scented summer dusk that seemed unlikely to get properly dark. The sky was so big here; there was so much space to float into. She began to think she'd feel shut in and streetbound if she had to go back to London, where the sky was all chopped up with wires and high buildings and street-lamps.

Greta's garden was taking shape. Will had finished planting the box hedges; on Monday, while Tizzie and Davy were at school, dozens more plants arrived from the nursery – lavender, clematis and a climbing rose – and Will spent the next two days planting those as well. On Friday, the dovecot and the marble bench were delivered. Will and Finnigan put them carefully into place, and now the garden was very nearly complete. All that was needed was for the doves to take up residence, and the plants to do some growing.

'Come and see!' Tizzie urged Mum, on Saturday after lunch.

Mum made a bored face. 'I've got chickens to joint for dinner. It's only a garden.'

'But a special one. Please come!'

Mum sighed, but followed Tizzie out into the sunshine.

In the Knot Garden they found Finnigan, checking yet again that everything was perfect; with a small dustpan and brush he was sweeping up spilled soil from the paving.

'Hello!' Tizzie called to him. 'I've brought Mum to see – look, Mum, isn't it lovely!' She mounted the two steps to the terrace where the new marble bench stood. 'You'll be able to sit here and watch the doves, and listen to them cooing –' She went to sit down, to demonstrate.

'No!' Finnigan's voice cut in, harsh and abrupt. He dropped the dustpan and brush with a clatter, then stepped towards her and took her arm, almost pushing her aside.

What had she done wrong? She gazed at him, hurt and startled.

'Sorry,' he said at once, letting go. 'I'm sorry, Tizzie – Morag. It's just – this is Greta's garden, you know.'

'I was only looking!'

Finnigan smoothed the clouded white marble with his hand. 'This has been made specially. Lord Rupert's instructions. No one must sit on it till Greta comes. Afterwards, maybe,' he conceded, 'if Greta doesn't mind.'

'Come on, Tizzie. We're not wanted here.' Ignoring Finnigan, Mum took hold of Tizzie's wrist and towed her out of the garden.

Tizzie balked, trying to dig her heels in, but Mum was stronger, and very determined. 'Mum, stop it! Let go of me!'

'No!' Mum said fiercely. 'I don't want you hanging around here. Making a nuisance of yourself.'

Tizzie looked back at Finnigan, expecting him to defend her, but he was too busy with his precious clematis, encouraging its leaf-stems to twine round the supports of the arch. With a furious shake and a twist, she managed to wriggle out of Mum's grasp. 'What's the matter with you? What's the matter with *him*? I was only—'

'He's a stupid old man, that's what's the matter!' Mum hissed, evidently not caring whether Finnigan heard or not.

'Mum! How can you be so horrible!'

'I'm just stating a fact. I've told you not to get in Finnigan's way. If you do, and he loses his rag, then don't come running to me for sympathy.'

'*Sympathy!* As if I would!' Tizzie flared. 'All I ever get from you is bad temper and blame and grumbling! At least Finnigan *likes* me. I mean, usually he does.' Her voice wavered. 'I wonder if you even like me at all!' Tears blurred her eyes; she turned and ran.

Where was she going? Not back to the Knot Garden – but as she swerved left to a brick path that led to the pond, she saw Finnigan walking towards her.

'Greta!' he called. 'I'm sorry—'

'I'm not *Greta!*' she flung back. 'Greta! Always Greta! Is she the only person that matters?'

Confusion flittered across his face. 'No – I – wait!'

'Oh, leave me alone!'

She veered away across the grass. They were mad, both of them, mad and horrible, as bad as each other! She'd only wanted to show Mum the garden. How had things gone so wrong, ending up in bad temper and shouting?

Tizzie trailed around the garden for a while, wondering if Davy might be about; but now she remembered that he'd gone down to the farm where Lee lived. She thought she might go to the paddock and see if Ditty was there, but when she saw the pony grazing by the hedge she changed her mind. Ditty was Greta's pony. The garden was for Greta. The dolls' house was for Greta. *Everything* was for Greta. Greta ought to be the happiest girl alive: it would be so easy to be happy, Tizzie thought, if you were Greta. Being happy and Tizzie seemed a lot, lot harder. Impossible, at times. Whenever she caught herself being happy, something would turn against her, and spoil it.

Without knowing quite what to do, she wandered back to Cloud Cottage and up to her room. She stared gloomily out of the window for a while, thought about writing to Kamila but wasn't in the mood, then heard banging and slamming from the room below. Mum's room.

Tizzie ran down to see what was going on.

Mum's holdall was on the bed. She was pulling clothes out of the wardrobe, stuffing them in: not bothering to fold them, just cramming them in anyhow.

'What are you *doing*?'

'What does it look like? I'm packing. We're going. Get your things together. We'll be out of here as soon as we can.'

'No! No!' Tizzie gripped the door-frame. 'You don't mean that! We can't go—'

'We can and we are.'

'But why? What's happened? You're supposed to be cooking. What about the chickens?'

'Stuff the chickens!' Mum gave a haughty toss of her pony-tail. 'I shouldn't have come here. It's too—'

'Too *what*?' Tizzie demanded, but Mum only pressed her lips together and shook her head. She slammed the door of the wardrobe and pulled out a drawer from the bedside table.

'I don't want to go! I *like* it here – Mum! Please! You can't do this!' Tizzie went to the bed and started hoiking clothes out of the bag as fast as Mum stuffed them in. She tossed socks, knickers and T-shirts in all directions: flung them into the air, scattered them over the floor.

'Tizzie! Stop it!' Mum pushed her away. 'You're behaving like a four-year-old!'

'And how d'you think *you're* behaving?' Tizzie shouted. 'This is crazy! Mad! You haven't given any *reason*. You said it'd be different this time – you said we'd stay! And you like it here, as much as you ever like anywhere—'

She thought of herself and Mum in the van, driving past the house, up the track and through the gates; turning away from Roven Mere, never to return. No! Leave Finnigan? Leave Greta, before they'd even met? Leave all the things she was waiting to find out?

Mum was darting about, gathering underwear. 'You'll go if I say so, Tizzie. Go upstairs and pack your things.'

'No! I won't! You can't make me. It's not fair to Finnigan.'

'What's Finnigan got to do with it?'

'Quite a lot!' Tizzie retorted. 'He's the one who gave you the job, isn't he? Or had you forgotten? What's he supposed to do now, if you walk out?'

'I don't give a toss about Finnigan!'

'Well, maybe you should! Is this all because he was rude just now? OK, he was, but no ruder than *you* are, all the time – rude and horrible and stupid—'

Mum stopped shoving things into the bag, and stood very still.

'Maybe I am,' she said quietly, 'but I've got my reasons.'

'*What* reasons? You haven't said anything that makes sense. You never do!'

'I've got reasons.' Mum glared defiance. 'You'll just have to take my word for it.'

'What about me?' Tizzie shouted. 'Do you ever think about me? Well, *I* do. *I* think about me! I want to stay here. I'm not going. I'm just not!'

'But I thought you—'

A loud thumping at the front door startled both of them. Tizzie looked at Mum, who made no move.

'I'll go, if you can't be bothered.' Tizzie ran down the stairs.

It was Finnigan who stood at the door.

'I've lost Small,' he said, and his face crumpled. 'I can't find him anywhere.'

21
The Turret Room

'I've searched everywhere,' Finnigan told Tizzie. 'The workshops, the courtyard, all over the garden.'

'I'll help! I bet he hasn't gone far.'

Tizzie ran down to the lake and looked in the boat-house, in case Small had curled up to sleep in the rowing-boat. Finnigan called Jack Doughty from where he'd been weeding the asparagus beds, and got him to check his flat above the stable.

'I haven't seen him since first thing this morning,' Finnigan kept saying. 'I'm afraid he's got shut in somewhere.'

'He's in the house, he must be,' said Davy, back from the farm.

'The well!' Finnigan said, aghast. 'What if he's fallen down the well? I should have covered it over – should have done it years ago—'

'Of course he hasn't!' Davy told him. 'He's not stupid.'

Finnigan insisted on going to look, though Tizzie didn't want to imagine what he expected to see.

'Come on, Tizzie,' said Davy. 'We'll find him, I bet.'

They ran up to the house. Glad to get away from Mum, and to put off any further argument, Tizzie was now overtaken by a new worry. What if something really *had* happened to Small? What if someone had taken him, or – awful thought – he'd gone as far as the road, and been run over? What if he were never seen again? Small was more to Finnigan than a cat, more than a pet. He was a companion, a friend. Already, she had seen Finnigan's dismay; he was dithery with shock. He mustn't lose Small.

'Where shall we start?' she asked Davy, as they approached the kitchen entrance. 'There are so many rooms!'

'One floor at a time. Lots of the rooms are locked, anyway.'

They went down the steps. Tizzie was wondering whether to say, if they met Mrs Crump, that Mum was at Cloud Cottage packing her bag, and there wouldn't be any dinner, nor any more meals at all; but to her astonishment she saw Mum at the kitchen table, preparing the chickens as if there had been no row, no shouting, no threats of leaving. The radio was on, and Mum humming along quite cheerfully.

'We're still looking for Small,' Tizzie told her. It was only because Davy was with her that she bothered to be even slightly polite.

'That cat?' Mum reached for the salt. 'Don't waste your time. It'll turn up when it feels like it. That's what cats are like.'

In spite of this discouragement, Tizzie's heart lifted. Mum must have changed her mind about leaving – for now, at any rate.

Davy and Tizzie went along the corridor, looking in all the store-rooms and cupboards, calling and calling. Up to the first floor they went, moving along the corridors, opening doors. There were rooms here that Tizzie hadn't yet seen: some with furniture shrouded in dust-sheets, others with beds made up, and flowers in vases. So many places for a cat to hide!

'We'll never find him.' Tizzie began to despair. 'He could be *any*where.'

'But he is *some*where,' Davy said. 'And of all the places he could be, he can only be in one of them. All we've got to do is find that place.'

Stairs, back stairs, cupboards under stairs, lumber-rooms, and that wasn't even including the attics. Tizzie began to feel quite lost; her study of the dolls' house hadn't shown her every twist of every corridor.

Up on the second floor, Davy paused on the landing.

'It'll take ages to go in every single room up here. Tell you what, I'll go this way, you go that way. Then we'll meet again back here. Yell if you see him.'

They were at the start of what Davy called the museum rooms. Tizzie opened one door after another, called inside, searched. Dolls. China and glass animals. Masks. Wood-carvings. An advent calendar made to look like a wooden house, with shutters that opened to reveal the pictures underneath.

Almost on tiptoes, walking as quietly as she could, Tizzie moved from room to room, from object to object, touching, examining, wondering. Wouldn't Greta be surprised to find that she had her very own museum! But it would be a lonely thing to do, exploring a museum all by herself. Wouldn't she be glad that Tizzie and Davy were here? We'll look at it all together, Tizzie decided, and I'll pretend not to have seen any of it before, so that it can be exciting and new.

She had reached the room with the puppet theatre in it. She pulled back the drapes, just in case Small had curled up inside to sleep, and found herself eye to eye with the woman puppet, her face big and red above the frilled bathing costume. The grinning mouth leered at her. Hastily she backed away, checked that there was nowhere else for a cat to hide, then moved on.

The boarded wooden floor was uneven up here, with dips and risings and strange creakings, so that it felt like being on a boat out at sea. How ancient the roof-beams were, how massive! Tizzie felt quite giddied when she thought of all the people who must have walked along this corridor – going to bed with their candles, perhaps, or servants getting up very early to light fires – and all the hopes and joys and worries that must have filled their heads. It would be a bit creepy to be up here alone in the dark, and even now, she was glad that Davy wasn't far away.

Rounding a corner, she came to a door set diagonally across the turn in the corridor. This door was a heavy wooden one like the others, but rather lower. The latch fastening lifted easily at her touch, and the door swung open inward.

She knew at once where she was. This was the turret! She'd seen it in miniature, but the dolls' house gave no glimpse of what might be inside. Now she was about to find out.

The room inside was round, lit only by daylight from a small diamond-paned window half-way up a flight of stairs that clung to the curve of the wall.

'Small!' Tizzie called softly.

There was no answering miaow. Seeing with a glance that there was no cat here, nor anywhere for one to hide, Tizzie crept slowly up the stairs. They were open-sided, with only a rope fastened to rings on the wall as a hand-rail. This tower, she thought, was exactly the sort of place where a princess in a fairy-tale might be kept imprisoned. Maybe even a whole family! With a shiver of excitement, she remembered what Lee Dingleby had told her. Could it be possible that Lord Rupert and his family were in hiding here? But why? And anyway, they were hardly being kept captive, with the door so easy to open.

Having expected the stairs to go up and up, Tizzie was disappointed when they ended in a small round room, identical to the one below. There was only a flat ceiling above – not even a trap-door. This room, with its window that looked out into the trees behind the house, was lined with bookshelves, a cupboard and a small desk made to fit into the curve of the wall. On the desk was a laptop computer. All was dusted and cleaned and ready.

Looking more closely at the books, Tizzie saw dictionaries, a set of encyclopaedia, a thesaurus, books about space and history and animals and how things work; there were CD ROMs in cases. It looked as if someone came here to do homework, and that someone could of course only be Greta. Tizzie's spirits lifted as she imagined herself and Greta sitting here together each evening – there would be room for two at the desk – helping each other with their school-work, bringing drinks and chocolate. If that computer had internet access, she could email Kamila as well, and feel that she was with both her friends at once. She stifled a twinge of resentment at this room being kept secret, ready for Greta and

Greta alone, when she and Davy could have been using it.

The cupboard under the desk had a small lock with a key in it. Opening it, Tizzie found school-books piled inside. She pulled them out, and knelt on the floor to look. There were exercise books in various colours: dark red, dark green, dark blue. Each one was printed on the cover with SANDITON SCHOOL FOR GIRLS, and underneath were the usual spaces for NAME, FORM and SUBJECT. Greta Evershall, Form 1A, was written on each book in blue ink-pen. *Greta Evershall, Mathematics. Greta Evershall, Domestic Science. Greta Evershall, English Composition.* And Science, French, R.E., Latin, History.

Tizzie's fingers trembled as she flicked open the French book. To see Greta's handwriting was a big step closer to meeting Greta herself!

It was obvious that Greta was good at French: red ticks scattered the pages, with a liberal garnishing of *très bien!* in a hand far less legible than Greta's. Maths was also very good, marked in green this time. Doubt frayed the edges of Tizzie's excitement. Greta was obviously the sort of girl who could sail through school work with ease. In Tizzie's case it was more like grappling at things she could barely understand, and trying to hide the things she didn't grasp at all. Greta would be bound to have clever friends at Sanditon School: friends like herself, sleek and confi-dent, who would come round for tea. Those girls would be the ones invited up here for chocolate and

164

secrets, and they'd be scornful of Tizzie for being dull and ordinary and not clever at all.

English Composition would tell her more than lists of French irregular verbs or pages of equations. Tizzie opened the book.

About Myself, said the title.

About Myself – that must be the first assignment, helping the English teacher to get to know her new class. Tizzie had written more *About Myself* pieces than she could count – almost every time she started at a new school, often parked in an office somewhere out of the way while the teachers decided what to do with her.

My name is Margareta Evershall, Tizzie read, *but nearly everyone calls me Greta. My father is Lord Rupert Evershall and my mother's name is Angelina, Angel for short. I live at Paradise Hall, near the village of Sleet, in Gloucestershire. We have lived here since I was five years old. I am an only child, and this is a very big old house, too big for the three of us. It takes a number of servants to look after it all. I would really like to have a brother or sister, but I don't think I ever will, now.*

Soon I will be twelve. I've got long fair hair but I wish I was prettier and taller. (Here, the teacher had put a line through *was*, and written *were – subjunctive,* in red in the margin.) *My parents have promised to buy me a pony, and I shall choose a dapple-grey one with a white mane and tail. When I have a pony of my very own, I shall be the luckiest girl in the world …*

Tizzie was hardly breathing while she read, as if too loud an exhalation might frighten Greta away. Now, as her eyes flicked back to the top of the page, she let out her breath in a huff of surprise. The date written there and neatly underlined was *15th September 1987.*

1987? What – the figures jumbled themselves into nonsense in Tizzie's brain – twenty years ago, more? Before she'd even been born? Her eyes had gone funny. It must be a mistake, surely—

'Tizzie!' yelled Davy's voice. 'Are you up there?'

Startled, unable to remember where she was and why, Tizzie closed the book and shoved it with the others into the cupboard. But her fingers would not quite let go of the English book. She still had it in her hand when she got to her feet and called back, 'Coming!' The cat, she thought. Of course, they were looking for Small.

'Thought you'd got lost!' Davy was standing inside the open door at the bottom of the stairs.

'Have you found him?'

'No! I've been everywhere I can think of.' He was looking at her as she came down the stairs, with the exercise book rolled into a tube and tucked under her arm. 'I haven't been in here for ages,' he added. 'If I lived in the house, I'd have this for my own bedroom, away from everyone. Is there anything up there?'

Tizzie hesitated. 'Not really – books, mainly. Where shall we look next?'

'He might have turned up by now. Let's go back to the caravan and see. If not, we'll look in the woods.'

They left the turret, and Tizzie turned to latch the door behind her.

'What's that you've got?' Davy asked.

'Just a book. I'm just borrowing it. I want to look at it properly later.'

'Whose book?'

Reluctantly, Tizzie showed him. 'Greta's. Look. Greta Evershall. But I just don't get it – see—' She pointed to the date on the first page. 'How can that make sense? Greta's twelve, we know she is. It must be a mistake.'

'Let's see.' Davy took the book, and flipped through the pages. 'No – October, November – it goes on as far as June, 1988. Then there's no more.'

'What does it mean?' Tizzie's mind was racing. 'Did Greta leave here all that time ago – when Roven Mere was called Paradise Hall?'

'No! That was another Lord Rupert, not this one. There must have been another Greta, as well.'

'Margareta, this one's name is, really.' Tizzie took the book back and showed him the first page. 'Greta was just her nickname. Maybe our Greta was named after her? But does that mean *two* Gretas have lived here? And she *sounds* like our Greta, with the long hair, and the dapple-grey pony – I mean – as far as—' She stopped in confusion. Which of the Gretas, if there were two, was she talking about? Whose portrait had she seen? Whose bedroom?

167

Davy seemed to have lost interest. 'There's nothing to say this other one *did* leave, is there? Anyway, there's a quick way to find out,' he added, leading the way back along the corridor. 'Ask Finnigan. He'll know.'

22

The Cellar Steps

'Here he is, the good boy, the bad chap!' said Finnigan, holding the cat in his arms. 'I was coming to find you.'

Small looked at Davy and Tizzie from under Finnigan's chin. Smug and sleepy, he stretched his claws, then yawned widely. Finnigan wore a weary smile that looked as if it could easily turn to tears.

'Where d'you find him?' Davy asked.

'I went up to the woods and called for him there, and by the time I got back he was in the caravan, in his usual place on the bench, fast asleep. He'd stayed out hunting, I bet, that was all. Thank you both for looking. I ought to know better than to get myself so worked up.' Finnigan stroked the cat fondly, adding, 'Silly old fool.'

Tizzie didn't know if he meant the cat, or himself. She felt rather deceived by Small. She'd been *anxious* about him, really worried, thinking of him as an innocent victim of a speeding driver or a cat-thief, or shut in somewhere to pine and starve. Now here he was, sleek, fat and unrepentant: not prey after all, but hunter.

'Oh well, that's all right.' Davy had already turned away, back towards the gardens. 'He's been after baby rabbits, I bet. I said I'd help Dad. D'you want to come, Tizz?'

'In a minute I will.'

She was still holding the exercise book; it felt glowing and alive, almost burning her hand. Finnigan was too overcome by Small's return to have noticed, and Davy had already forgotten about it. But Tizzie had to *know*.

She waited while Finnigan went into the caravan and opened a tin of pilchards for Small, carefully turning over the halves of fish and forking out the small bones. Small was to be given a reward for being bad, for giving everyone such trouble. Purring loudly, the cat hunkered over the saucer and began to bolt down the fishy chunks. Finnigan sat on the bench to watch him, adoringly. He seemed to have forgotten that Tizzie was there.

He loves Small, she thought. Finnigan loves Small.

And that makes him happy, but, always, at risk of being *un*happy. This small sad thought stirred up her own feeling of loss – every time she thought she was getting closer to Greta, something happened to take her away again.

Twenty years away? No, impossible.

Tizzie went to the caravan doorway and stood on the step. She cleared her throat. 'Finnigan,' she said, and held out the exercise book. 'I found this. It's Greta's. But look at the date. September 1987. I don't get it – how can Greta's school book be dated twenty years ago?'

Finnigan's expression changed. Tizzie had heard of people turning pale with shock, but never till now had she seen someone actually *do* it. Finnigan stared at the book, at the page she showed him, and the colour seemed to drain out of his face, leaving it grey.

'Where did you get this?' he asked, his voice husky.

Tizzie explained. While she was talking, Finnigan continued to hold the book in shaking hands, staring at it. She couldn't tell whether he took in what she said, any of it at all. Before she'd even finished, he got up without a word, crossed the yard to his workshop, and slid the door shut, leaving her outside.

Small had finished his pilchards, every last scrap. With his saucer now licked shining clean, he sat washing his paws in the sunshine.

'Finnigan!' Tizzie called. 'Can't I come in? I want to ask you something!'

No answer. She tried opening the door, but found

it firmly closed from inside; she stood with her ear pressed to it, listening. 'Finnigan!' she called again. Not a sound. Not even the tapping of a hammer or the sound of rummaging through tools, to suggest that he was at work.

What was he *doing* in there?

Giving up, Tizzie went in search of Davy, to tell him what had happened. But she found only Jack Doughty, digging up new potatoes. Davy and Will had gone off in Will's van to buy wood preservative and paint, he told her. 'And your mam's making a special dinner for tonight. You can pick the fruit if you like.'

'A special dinner? What for?' Considering that Mum had been ready to pack up and leave only a few hours ago, Tizzie found this hard to believe.

'She din't say. Only she wants potatoes, broad beans and peas and gooseberries. You can pick the goose-gogs if you like.'

'Is it for *them*? Have they come early?' Hope leaped again.

'She din't say. Here. You can put them in this trug.'

Jack gave her a sort of flat wooden basket, and showed her the gooseberry bushes, planted in a row along the edge of the vegetable plot. 'Mind them spikes,' he warned. 'Vicious, they are if you don't watch out. Don't go sticking your hand in without looking.'

Tizzie hadn't seen gooseberries growing on bushes, and wasn't sure she'd ever eaten them. The fruits were fat and bristly, golden-green, warm to the touch. She picked and picked, putting one into her mouth and tasting its curious sharp green sweetness. This was turning into such a peculiar day that she wouldn't have thought it odd if a troupe of circus performers had arrived on the lawn. Mum threatening to leave, then deciding instead to cook a grand dinner! Finnigan behaving so weirdly at the sight of an old school-book! What was the *matter* with them? Perhaps, she thought, it's this *place*. It gets hold of people and scrambles their brains.

The special dinner, though! Were Lord Rupert and Greta coming home tonight? But how could Mum *know*, if Finnigan didn't? He hadn't mentioned it, had shown no sign of excitement – but perhaps that was because of the Small-hunt. Tizzie imagined the long table set properly, with candles lit; the dumb-waiter running smoothly up its shaft, loaded with Mum's delicious-smelling dinner. At the top there'd be someone very smartly dressed – Finnigan, it would have to be, unless Mrs Crump did waitressing – to carry the food to the table and bring away the empty dishes. At the end of the meal, Finnigan would say to Greta, 'Now, there's someone who's been looking forward to meeting you,' and Greta would exclaim with delight, and the friendship would begin. Then none of the confusion over dates and school-books would matter in the slightest, because everything would soon be explained.

Wanting to see exactly what Mum was up to, Tizzie offered to take all the fruit and vegetables up to the kitchen, but Jack Doughty said it was too much for her to carry, so they both went. Tizzie felt almost as proud as if she'd grown it all herself: the small, firm potatoes with their rich earth coating; the gooseberries like fat fuzzy beads ready to be strung on a necklace; the peas and beans still snug and secret in their pods.

Mum was darting about busily: checking the oven, bringing out scales, lining up serving dishes. She hummed cheerfully along with the radio as she worked. She looked happily engrossed.

'Is the table laid?' Tizzie asked.

'You can see it isn't!' Mum plonked down a measuring-jug. 'That can wait till later. I need the space.'

'No, I meant – won't they be eating upstairs?'

Mum gave her an odd look. 'They? There's no *they*. It'll be the same people as usual.'

'Oh.' Tizzie's spirits flopped again. 'So what's the special occasion?'

'There isn't an occasion! I just felt like making a bit of an effort, OK?' Mum snapped, then, seeming to realise how harsh she'd sounded, she said it again, much more nicely. 'I thought I'd make a bit of an effort. For us all. See, look, I've done a special menu.' She indicated the card pinned to the cork notice-board, written by hand and decorated with a leafy border. Tizzie read:

> *Broad beans with lemon and dill,*
> *pitta and olives*
>
> *Chicken with garlic and white wine*
> *Buttered new potatoes*
> *Fresh peas*
>
> *Gooseberry Fool with brandysnap biscuits*

'Sounds yummy,' Tizzie said, her voice hollow with disappointment. Perhaps this was a practice run.

'It'd be great if you felt like helping!' Mum gave an uncertain smile. 'How about topping and tailing those gooseberries? I'll show you how.'

Tizzie looked at her. What was going on? But she didn't want Mum's mood to turn again, so the question bursting to be asked, *what's changed your mind?* stayed unspoken. Taking the role of kitchen assistant: she prepared the fruit, washed the potatoes, and finally set the table. She didn't see anyone other than Mum and Mrs Crump, who kept coming in and sniffing and saying 'My, we're in for a real treat!' Just before seven, Mum took off her apron and brushed her hair and even put on a little make-up, which she hardly ever bothered with. She grimaced at her reflection in the hand-mirror, and seemed embarrassed when she saw Tizzie looking at her.

'Just making a bit of an effort, like I said.' She sounded defensive, even though Tizzie hadn't said a word.

Tizzie's suspicions sharpened. Was this all for Will Crump's benefit – the make-up, the special menu?

Mum fussed around the table, tweaking a napkin here, aligning a fork there. She found soft music on the radio. People started to come in – Jack Doughty, Will and Davy, Mrs Crump. Word must have got around, because Will Crump was wearing a tie and a clean-looking shirt, and Jack Doughty had put on a jacket in horrendous maroon checks, with a cravat of spotted green. Mrs Crump was wearing an orange-flowered dress that billowed around her ankles, and bright pink lipstick that clashed.

It was funny, seeing them dressed-up and self-conscious, but Tizzie wished she'd known; she could have worn something other than the blue top she'd had on all day. Mum was in T-shirt and jeans as usual, but Tizzie noticed now that she was wearing a necklace: a peacock-blue gemstone in the shape of a teardrop, on a slender silver chain. Tizzie's eyes fastened on it in puzzlement. She hadn't seen that before – where had it come from? Mum would never buy jewellery for herself. Could Will have given it to her? Mum wouldn't catch Tizzie's eye; she was flushed and a little flustered.

Everyone was here except Finnigan. His place, at the head of the table, was empty.

'I said seven o'clock,' Mum said, refolding a napkin.

'He's late.'

'He'll be on his way.' Will Crump gave her a big, reassuring grin. 'Davy, why don't you nip down and hurry him along? Tell him we're all ready.'

Davy went; everyone waited. Will uncorked a bottle of wine, and Tizzie fetched drinks from the fridge for herself and Davy. Mum checked the chickens, letting out a fragrant waft from the oven. Jack Doughty kept saying that this would certainly be worth waiting for.

'Will's off out for the day tomorrow,' Mrs Crump announced, when the conversation faltered. 'Taking his lady friend to a flower show.'

'Oh, ah,' said Jack Doughty. He nudged Will with his elbow, as if a naughty secret had just been let out. 'That's that young woman lives over Shadway, is it?'

Will smiled and nodded. 'That's right. Gillian.'

'Been seeing each other six months now, they have,' Mrs Crump said, smilily.

Tizzie's eyes flew to Mum. *Lady friend!* A lady friend called Gillian, barging in and spoiling her theory! But Mum seemed unperturbed; she was lifting a saucepan lid to check the potatoes, turning down the heat. 'Oh! Why didn't you say? You could have invited her over!' she said to Will. 'There's more than enough food.'

Davy's feet could be heard running down the cellar steps.

'He's not coming. He said sorry but he's not coming.'

'Why not?' said Mum, crossly.

'He didn't say. It took ages before he came to the caravan door. It was all shut up – I wasn't even sure he was in there. The curtains were closed.'

'Is he ill, then?' asked Mum. 'Or what?'

'Best just to leave him be,' Mrs Crump told her. 'He'll get over it. Let's not spoil your lovely meal.'

But Mum went sulky-faced. She served the starter – a herby lemony dip, green and mashy – with ill grace, plonking the plates down in front of people. Warm pitta bread was passed round, cut into small strips.

Everyone tried to make up for Finnigan's absence.

'Oooh, delicious!'

'What did you call it, again?'

'Never thought olives agreed with me, but these are fantastic.'

Next the chicken, fragrant and garlicky, tender enough to slide away from the bones. More enthusiasm: 'Your own recipe, is this?'

'Mmm! Is there any more going?'

'Nothing like peas freshly podded from your own garden, I always say.'

'New potatoes, all buttery, nothing to beat 'em.'

'Glad you like it,' Mum said flatly.

'Best meal I've had for years! I couldn't eat another thing – but what's this? Gooseberry fool? Well, I won't say no—'

Tizzie tried hers, and tasted sunshine and rain and the garden, the cream laced with sharpness. Mmmm.

'You're quiet, Tizzie,' Will Crump said, across the

table. 'You ought to have some of the credit, didn't you? You've been helping.'

Tizzie wasn't sure she could forgive him for having a Lady Friend who wasn't Mum. She gave a dutiful smile, but said nothing.

Nearly everyone had seconds. Jack Doughty licked the back of his spoon. 'Finnigan dun't know what he's missing.'

'We could have saved him some,' said Davy.

Tizzie's mum gave a little shake of her head. 'Don't see why. Not if he can't be bothered to show his face. He can make himself a sandwich if he's hungry.'

'Are you sure he'll be all right?' Tizzie asked Mrs Crump.

'He has these funny moods, dear. Throwing himself into his work like he does – sometimes it all gets a bit much. Specially now, with the Evershalls coming so soon.'

The last gooseberry sweetness slithered down Tizzie's throat. 'So they really are coming?' The words were out of her mouth before she'd planned to say them.

Mrs Crump's eyebrows shot up into the stiff waves of her hair; then she laughed. 'I certainly hope so, lovey! It's what we're all here for, isn't it?'

Jack Doughty nodded. 'It'll be just like the old days.'

'But while we've still got the place to ourselves, it's lovely to have a bit of a party.' Mrs Crump delved into a capacious bag beside her chair, and produced a box of mint chocolates. 'Look, I got us these, to have with our coffee.'

'How'll they get here?' Tizzie asked. 'The Evershalls? If they've been travelling?'

'That I don't know.' Mrs Crump peeled off the cellophane wrapper. 'Finnigan hasn't said whether they're flying back or coming by train or boat. They'll hire a car, I suppose, unless they want Will to drive and fetch them from somewhere. It'll be nice for Greta to have you two here.' She looked at Davy and then at Tizzie, passing the mints. 'Lonely old place this'd be for a young girl, else. I've often thought that. It's different for Davy – he's got his friends in the village.'

'Greta?' Jack Doughty looked puzzled. 'Is she coming back, then?'

'Yes, Jack, you know she is,' Mrs Crump told him clearly; then added, in a lower voice, 'He gets confused. Forgets what day of the week it is, sometimes.'

Tizzie didn't think it was polite to talk about Jack Doughty as if he weren't here. Jack smiled and nodded, but still looked confused.

'Things'll be a lot different,' said Will Crump, unwrapping a mint, and twisting the shiny green wrapper into a snake. 'You know, I've got so used to them not being around – always expected, never actually turning up – I sort of forget they exist. It's like we're running the place just for ourselves. And in a way I prefer it like this.'

'I do, too,' said Davy. 'I don't even want them to come.'

'Just listen to the pair of you!' Mrs Crump sat back

in her chair. 'You'd better get used to some big changes. Running the place just for ourselves! Who pays our wages? Who pays for all this?' She waved a hand, indicating the remains of the meal.

'I know, I know.' Will gave a sheepish smile.

'Me, I'm looking forward to seeing the house properly lived-in,' Mrs Crump went on. 'Seems all wrong to have this big place empty like it is, with just us rattling round in it. It'll be just like old times, as you say, Jack. Dinner parties, guests staying and the like.'

'Rich people,' Will said. 'They're not like us.'

'Oh, I don't know,' said Mrs Crump. 'People are all the same under the skin.'

'Are they?' Mum said abruptly. 'It seems to me that people are different and surprising.'

Everyone looked at her, expecting more. Mum looked embarrassed; she got up from the table and busied herself refilling the coffee-pot.

'Yes, you're right, of course,' said Mrs Crump, smiling, smoothing over what had somehow become an awkward moment. 'The same but different. That's what I meant, really.'

Tizzie was fiddling with a teaspoon. She held it up and saw her own face distorted and lengthened in it, clown-like. She was thinking of the friendly Greta she thought she knew, and the ever-absent Greta she didn't really know in the slightest. Mum said she'd be disappointed. Davy said Greta would be a spoilt little cow. What if she was? She was a rich girl, with a pony of her own, and a mansion to live in. She won't want me for her friend, Tizzie thought. Why did I ever imagine she would?

The mints went round the table a second time. The grown-ups seemed in no hurry to leave; they sat drinking their coffee, talking and laughing. Tizzie began to feel fidgets in her legs and bottom; Davy caught her eye, gesturing *Shall we go out?* They both pushed back their chairs.

'Remember your manners!' Will said sharply to Davy.

'Oh. Yeah. Thanks, Morag, for the dinner. It was really great,' Davy said, prompting a new chorus of 'Certainly was,' 'Better than those TV chefs, you are,' and 'What a feast!'

Tizzie and Davy went up the cellar steps into the fading glow of the evening. The sky was streaked pink and purple; it felt as if it would never get properly dark. There was a kind of surprise and tingle in the air. Looking up, Tizzie saw the flicker and tumble of dark shapes against the sky, up near the roof-eaves.

'Look!' She pointed. 'What are they?'

Davy stood on the top step, hands in pockets, head tilted back. 'Bats! We get them here sometimes on summer nights.'

Tizzie gazed. Bats! Real bats! They weren't much like the solid black cut-outs of Hallowe'en decorations. They were fast and faint, so quick that her eyes could barely catch them – they swooped and wheeled, then she had the briefest sense of a ragged flutter before they soared again and were lost in the deepening blue.

'You needn't worry,' Davy told her. 'They won't get tangled up in your hair. Some people think that, but it's rubbish. Bats are brilliant fliers.'

'I'm not scared,' said Tizzie. 'Just watching.'

She remembered Finnigan. It seemed heartless that they'd all been eating and enjoying themselves, having a party, while he was shut up alone with his misery. But she pushed him out of her thoughts. The beauty of the midsummer evening made her want to fly with the bats, up in the cool air, under the first emerging stars.

23

Nevermore

In the morning, as soon as she'd had breakfast, Tizzie went down to the caravan. She hoped she'd find Finnigan busy and cheerful in his workshop as if nothing had happened, but instead the doors were still locked, the caravan shut up, the curtains closed.

What now? She couldn't just go away again. Was he in there or not?

She tapped lightly on the door. 'Finnigan!' she called. No answer, but then she heard a scrabbling from inside, and a faint miaowing. If Small was in the Dove-Grey Tourer, probably Finnigan was, too.

Maybe he hadn't even come out since yesterday evening.

What if something awful had happened? What if he'd *died* in there?

'Finnigan!' Tizzie called, and rapped more loudly. 'It's me – Tizzie!'

She heard a creaking sound, and then a heavy tread coming towards her. Bolts slid back. Finnigan opened the door. He gazed at her as if he'd never seen her before. He looked old and grey and ill. His face was bristly, and a stale musty smell wafted out of the caravan. He was wearing the same tweedy clothes as usual, but it looked as if he'd slept in them.

'What's the matter?' Tizzie tried. 'I came to see how you are. I was worried. Aren't you well? Should I tell Mrs Crump to get a doctor?'

Still he didn't speak. His mouth moved but no words came out. He must have lost his voice.

'Have you had any breakfast? Did you eat anything yesterday? Shall I make you a cup of tea? If you let me in, I'll make you one.'

Finnigan made a small sound, a moaning, protesting kind of sound, but then his mouth moved again and words came out. 'I can do that. You sit down and I'll put the kettle on.'

Tizzie went in, and sat on the bench by the little table. It was the first time she'd actually been in the caravan. When she'd glanced in before, everything had been neat and clean. Now the bed was rumpled, though it looked as if Finnigan had lain on top of it rather than in it. A fly buzzed round Small's food-bowl on the floor. While Finnigan filled the kettle, the cat rubbed itself against his legs, purring.

'Haven't I even fed you yet?' Finnigan muttered. When he'd lit the gas ring for the kettle, he opened a tin of cat-food and forked meat into a clean dish.

He made two mugs of tea, and sat down in silence. He'd made it very strong, but Tizzie didn't want to risk upsetting him by not drinking it. She wondered what to do next.

'Have you got any more stories?' she asked him, just for something to say.

He paused, looked at the floor, looked at the ceiling, then said, 'Yes. Yes, I have got one. Do you want to hear it, though?'

'Yes, please.'

Finnigan sighed, swigged at his tea, then put his mug down on the table. 'It goes like this:

Once there was a man who wanted to know what happiness was, and how to find it—'

'Don't you know any other beginnings? We've had that one,' Tizzie objected. 'Twice. There was Peregrine, and there was Thaddeus.'

'Yes, but listen. Once there was a man who wanted to know what happiness was, and how to find it, and his name was Rupert.'

'Lord Rupert?' Tizzie sat forward eagerly.

'Lord Rupert, that's right. Though he wasn't Lord Rupert at first, of course. He was only Lord Rupert after his father died. Well, soon Rupert had every reason to think himself the luckiest and happiest man in the whole world. He had a lovely wife called Angel, and he had a beautiful little girl—'

'Greta!' said Tizzie.

'—called Greta. Yes. She was christened Margareta, but soon her parents called her Greta, because they liked it. It reminded Lord Rupert of Gretel in the Hansel and Gretel fairy story, but what he should have remembered, of course, is that Gretel got lost. Lost in the woods.'

'But she came back again at the end,' Tizzie said. 'Nannina used to read it to me when I was little. The witch tried to eat her and Hansel, but they were clever. They found a way to escape.'

Where was the story going? Was he going to tell her that Greta had got lost in a forest and trapped by a witch?

'This Greta escaped, too,' said Finnigan. 'But not from a witch. Rupert, as I said, had every reason to be thankful. Not only did he have his wife Angel and his little girl Greta, but they lived in a beautiful old house called Paradise Hall—'

'That's here, isn't it?' Tizzie said. 'Roven Mere.'

'We'll come to that. They lived in a beautiful old house called Paradise Hall, in a wooded valley looking down at a lake. All around them the country-side stretched for miles and miles. The only sadness for Rupert and his wife was that as the years went by, there was no sign of a baby brother or sister for Greta. When Rupert came to live in such a big house, he imagined it full of children, full of happy voices, full of games and mischief.

So he lavished all his love on Angel and Greta. He did everything he could think of to make them happy. He made gardens and bowers and fountains, he bought a pony for Greta, he planned to make a little boat so that they could go rowing on the lake. He employed the best servants and the best cooks. Nothing was too much trouble for Rupert—'

Tizzie nodded. 'This is the old Greta, isn't it? The one whose school book I found? Not the one who's coming home now?'

'Wait,' Finnigan said sternly. 'Wait. Nothing was too much trouble for Rupert, and nothing too good for his wife and daughter. And for a while they were happy.'

'What spoiled it?'

'Rupert did,' Finnigan replied. 'Rupert spoiled it. He wanted to do everything for them. He loved them too much.'

'But how could he—'

'He loved them too much,' Finnigan repeated. 'He loved not wisely but too well. He smothered them with his own wants for them. Until Angel felt trapped like a bird in a cage, unable to stretch her wings, even to sing. So she went away, taking Greta with her.'

'Went away? Where? Went away without him?'

'They went away, he had no idea where. He was left all alone in his splendid house – left alone with his servants, that is, and all the things he'd bought. He couldn't rest till he'd searched for his wife and his little girl. He travelled far and wide, the length and breadth of England and beyond. He went to other countries, he searched and searched until it became quite pointless. He tried to guess where they might have gone. He made wilder and wilder guesses, all of them wrong. He asked in every city, every town and village he came to. And the more he searched, the more hopeless it seemed.

He spent a year searching, finding no trace of them. And then he came home.

Never was there a more wretched, desolate man. The name Paradise Hall seemed like a mockery, so he changed it to Roven Mere.'

'Why that?' asked Tizzie. 'Where did he get that name?'

'He was brokenhearted,' Finnigan said simply. 'He was a wealthy man still – he could afford to buy anything he wanted. But that couldn't begin to console him. Now he'd lost everything he loved best, and didn't know where to find it. So he decided that never more would he love. Never more would he risk losing what he loved most. Never more would he put himself at risk. Never more, never more, never more. It became his refrain.' Finnigan looked at Tizzie. 'Don't you see? Nevermore. Roven Mere. A name that would always remind him. A name that was his protection from harm.'

'The boat,' Tizzie said. 'That's the name of the boat.'

'Yes.'

'Is it true, then?'

'Yes, it is,' said Finnigan.

'So where are they? How does the story end?'

There was a silence. Then: 'It has ended,' Finnigan told her. 'That was the end.'

Tizzie shook her head. 'No. No. That won't do. It needs a better ending. Like your last one did.'

'Go on, then, Tizzie.' Finnigan smiled sadly. 'See if you can do better.'

'Well, I'll try,' she said. But how? Stories could be dangerous, she saw that now. You never knew where they might go. They could lead you to a place of no hope, no future, a place you'd never escape from, because you'd simply give up trying. And it felt different, this time. With Thaddeus, in the other story, what she'd done was steer him away from the dead end he'd made, and given him another chance. Could she do that now, for Rupert?

But Rupert's story was about real people, so it felt important to get it right. Right? Truthful? But where *was* truth, and how could she possibly find it, in all the muddle of clues and hints, wild guesses and odd glimpses? And if she made something up, wouldn't it be a lie? Wouldn't it only mislead, with false hope?

The only thing to do was to start talking, and hope a story would tell itself.

'Greta was very sad, too,' she improvised. 'Because although she and her mother had plenty of money, and they could go wherever they wanted, she knew that her father loved her and would be missing her very badly. "When are we going home?" she kept asking her mother. And her mother – Angel, that is – would say "Soon." But *soon* never came.

They nearly always stayed at the seaside, because Angel liked sunbathing and swimming in the sea. Every week Angel would give Greta her pocket-money, to spend on whatever she liked. But Greta never spent any of it. She saved it all up, and kept it in her purse. When her purse was bulging with coins, she put the money in a sock in her drawer. And when that sock was full up, she started on another one, till she had hardly any socks left to wear.

It was summer, and she thought of the garden at home, all pale with roses, and – and the bats flying above the cellar steps. And she felt so homesick, she thought she might actually die of it.

Most afternoons they went down to the beach. Greta would wander along by the edge of the sea, looking for shells, and things washed up by the tide. One day she saw a boy painting a blue rowing-boat. He painted it dark blue, and when he'd finished, he painted a name on the side, in yellow letters. NEVERMORE. Greta said the name aloud, and it made her sad. "Never more will I see my father again," she thought to herself. "Never more will I see Paradise Hall. Unless I do something."

One hot day, when Angel was asleep in her deckchair, Greta wrote a note on a postcard, and left it propped up in the sand. All it said was, *I've gone*

back to Paradise Hall. You can come too if you want. And she walked to the train station with her bundle of socks, and counted out the money for her fare, all in five pence pieces. The ticket-seller was a bit surprised, but she had enough, so she got her ticket and off she went. She had to change trains in London, and she had to walk miles at the other end. But all the time, she was getting closer to Paradise Hall. And home she came, just like a homing pigeon.'

Tizzie had a feeling that there ought to be more, but while she was wondering, Finnigan said, 'Did she really?'

'Yes, she did.'

'And stayed?'

'Yes, she stayed,' said Tizzie, 'and of course Angel came looking for her, and she stayed as well. And soon they wondered why they'd ever wanted to leave.'

Finnigan was silent for a few moments; then he gave a heavy sigh. 'Yes. It's a much better ending than mine. But I don't know if it could really happen like that.'

Neither did Tizzie. 'But your ending doesn't make sense,' she told him. 'You didn't say anything about Lord Rupert leaving again. Did he have another go at looking for them? Is that where he is now? Is that why—'

Finnigan held up a hand to make her stop talking. He looked old and ill. With his eyes closed, he said, 'Tizzie. I think Lord Rupert has been pretending. Pretending to himself. Pretending to everyone. Greta won't be coming back. Not really.'

'Has he said so? Have you seen him? How can you know?'

The words *Is she dead?* were leaping wildly in Tizzie's head. She couldn't ask, for fear of getting an answer. And if the answer should be *Yes,* the next question was already forming: *Did you kill her?* But why would he? Finnigan, who only talked about finding happiness, and losing it again? He wasn't a *killer.* That was just a stupid idea of Lee Dingleby's.

'You see – Tizzie, the truth is—' Finnigan began. Then a tread outside made them both jump, and a figure appeared in the doorway.

Mum.

Tizzie closed her eyes in exasperation. She had no idea what had brought Mum here, but now she'd be cross, and there'd be a big telling-off, ending with Tizzie being sent back to Cloud Cottage – just when she was poised on the edge of discovery!

Mum didn't look cross, though. All she said was, 'Oh, Tizzie. You're here. I thought you might be.' She turned to Finnigan, smiling. 'I just came to see if you're OK. We missed you last night.'

'Yes. I'm sorry,' Finnigan said gruffly. Then he lifted his head and stared straight at Mum. Tizzie looked, too. With her hair loose and brushed out, Mum looked younger and prettier than usual; or perhaps it was because she wasn't fierce or disapproving, but was smiling quite pleasantly. She looked almost embarrassed, without the grumpiness she usually wore like a suit of armour. She was wearing that necklace again, the one Tizzie hadn't seen till yesterday. Its stone of peacock-blue caught and held the light; that was what Finnigan was staring at.

'Where did you get that?' he snapped. 'That necklace?'

Mum stepped backwards off the step.

'Come with me and I'll tell you,' she said, in a teasing way.

Finnigan got up, barging against the table, sloshing the dregs of tea. 'You'll tell me, all right!' he shouted. He blundered down the step. 'When did you take that? How dare you?'

Tizzie couldn't believe how suddenly things had changed. What was going on? Mum, walking very fast, was already on the track, heading back towards the house. Finnigan stumbled after her.

'She stole it!' he rumbled, as Tizzie caught up with him. 'Stole it! Her! Stole!'

'But Mum wouldn't—'

'She can pack her bags and go,' Finnigan raged, at Mum's briskly walking back view. 'Now. Today. I'm not having a thief in the house. No thieves! There's too much to take.'

'She'll explain. She doesn't steal!' Tizzie was nearly running to keep up. 'She wouldn't!'

Instead of heading towards the house, or turning right for Cloud Cottage, Mum veered sharp left, up into the gardens. Along the narrow brick path she went, past the well-house, through the rose-walk.

Finnigan strode after her, outraged and indignant; Tizzie trotted behind. Mum seemed to be making for the Knot Garden. What was she *doing*? Mum wouldn't steal – would she? At this rate she'd get herself sacked, and they'd both be thrown out – Tizzie saw them on the road again, in the van, with nowhere to go, and let out a sob of exasperation. Why couldn't anything go *right*? Ever?

And why was Mum behaving so peculiarly? She seemed to have made a point of being nice to Finnigan, coming down specially to see him, only in order to upset and taunt him. This seemed even more obvious when Mum walked the length of the garden, mounted the steps to the clematis arch, and then sat – very deliberately, as if wanting to be watched – on the marble bench, Greta's marble bench. She sat in the middle of it, facing Finnigan and Tizzie across the box hedges and the lavender.

'What—' At first, Finnigan seemed barely able to speak. 'What do you—'

'Mum!' Tizzie yelled. 'Get off! You know you're not allowed to sit there – it's for Greta. Only for Greta!'

It was pointless, she knew that. Finnigan had said that Greta wasn't coming. But she had to keep pretending, if only for his sake.

Mum crossed one leg over the other, and sat smiling.

'Haven't you realised?' she called to them. 'Haven't you worked it out, either of you? Greta is me. I'm Greta. I've come home.'

Tizzie's eyes blurred. The lawn seemed to dip and sway under her feet. She must be sleepwalking.

'No. No,' said Finnigan. His voice came out as a croak.

'Yes, Dad. It's me,' said Mum. 'Really me.'

Dad? *Dad?*

Mum saw Tizzie's look of open-mouthed bewilderment.

'Yes, Tizz. It's him,' she said, and laughed. 'This is my father. Lord Rupert Evershall. Your grandfather.'

24
The Marble Bench

Tizzie felt as if she'd been painstakingly putting together a jigsaw, piece by piece, and then someone had come along and tipped it all to the floor in a jumbled, broken heap. When she began to put it together again, it made a different picture entirely: a new picture to dazzle and delight her. And each piece had its own story to tell.

She felt dizzier and fizzier and whizzier than she'd ever felt in her life before – her mind flashing with sparks, whirling in wonder. She was floating in a dream that seemed to be her real life. Her new real life.

'You knew?' she asked Mum. 'All the time?'

'Yes, I knew,' said Mum – this flushed, smiling Mum, this Morag who was Greta as well. 'As soon as I saw Roven Mere, when I came for the interview – as soon as I saw my father – Finnigan. That's why I took the job. Why we've come here.'

They were sitting in a row on Greta's bench, Mum in the middle. There had been laughing. There had been disbelief. There had been exclaiming and explaining, over and over again. There had been a bit of crying. There had been an awkward attempt at hugging, but neither Mum nor Finnigan were good huggers. It seemed easier just to sit together and let the questions come.

'But – why didn't you say?'

'I – I just couldn't,' said Mum. 'I had to live here and see what it was like. I had to get to know my father again. Get to know *myself.* The me that was and the me that is. Do you know what I mean, Tizzie?'

'I think so,' Tizzie said slowly. Yes, there was more than one Mum, just as, perhaps, there was more than one of everybody. She turned to Finnigan. 'But why do you call yourself Finnigan?'

Finnigan smiled. 'I think we've all done some name-changing. But Finnigan is one of my middle names. My full name is Rupert Raymond Finnigan Fraser Evershall, can you believe that? What an absurd bundle of names for one dull and unimportant person.'

'But you're *not*—' Tizzie protested.

'Finnigan seemed a lot simpler. And you, my dear?' Finnigan said to Tizzie's Mum. 'Tell Tizzie your names.'

'Margareta Elizabeth Evershall,' Mum answered.

'M.E.E.,' said Tizzie. 'MEE!'

'—Yes, I'm really MEE. When we left, I decided to be Margo for a bit. I had to leave Greta behind. We went from place to place, so I could call myself whatever I liked. Then I just changed the letters round a bit, and made Morag. I've been Morag since I was sixteen.'

'The house changed its name as well,' Tizzie remembered. 'But – Nannina?'

'Nannina!' Finnigan exclaimed. 'You've told me about her – I never for one moment guessed—'

'Nannina,' said Mum, 'is Angel. Angelina. Nina. We've all done it.'

'So she—'

Finnigan nodded sadly. 'Yes. It was like my story.'

'But the only story I had, over the years,' said Mum, 'was the one I got from her.'

'Tell us,' pleaded Tizzie.

'Well—' Mum gave an apologetic look to Finnigan, who nodded. 'This is how she told it to me. Her dream was to be an actress. She wanted to be on the stage, in plays in London. She met – Rupert Evershall, and they fell in love and decided to get married. At first they lived in a smart house in London, and she liked that – that's where I was born. Then the old Lord Rupert – my grandfather – died, and now Rupert, *this* Rupert, my father Rupert, became Lord Rupert. Then the move to the country, and this huge place. Paradise Hall, it was called then—'

'I know,' said Tizzie.

'And,' Finnigan broke in, 'she was unhappy here, as I should have guessed she would be. That was my mistake. I wanted a house full of children, but there were no more children. I thought what I wanted, *she* wanted. But I was wrong.'

'She wanted London, and parties, and fashion, and the theatre,' said Mum. 'The life she was used to. She didn't feel she belonged here. The summer I was twelve, she told me we were leaving. In secret. And that's what we did, on the twenty-eighth of June.'

'Oh!' Tizzie exclaimed. 'Thursday! That's what the anniversary is! I thought you meant a *happy* anniversary,' she reproached Finnigan.

He smiled. 'From now on it will be. We'll move it forward. We'll celebrate today, and this day every year will be a very special day indeed. Greta-and-Tizzie Day.'

Tizzie turned on her mother. 'But how could Nannina *do* that? Walk out and leave poor Rupert – poor Finnigan! Poor—'

She stopped in confusion. She'd been about to say Grandfather, but it didn't sound right. What was she going to call him? Grandfather, Gramps, Grandad? Pop, which was what Kamila called *her* grandfather? Finnigan was going to need another new name. 'Poor *you,'* she said, leaning across Mum to touch his arm. He took her hand, and held it briefly.

'I know. I know now,' said Mum. 'I didn't know then. She'd made me believe you were unfair and unkind. I'm sorry. More than I know how to say.'

Tizzie could never remember Mum saying sorry before, not to anyone.

'But maybe I was,' Finnigan said, huskily. 'Anyway, it wasn't *your* fault. Go on. And then?'

'We went to London. We stayed in cheap hotels, and Angel looked for work in theatres,' said Mum. 'But the problem was, she couldn't really act, or dance, or sing. It was just a dream. So she became wardrobe mistress, working for touring companies. We were always on the road, going from one small-town theatre to another.'

Tizzie nodded. 'She told me that bit.'

'She dyed her hair black, and it stayed black till she decided she was old enough to have it silver. She knew you'd come looking,' Mum told Finnigan, 'but she was determined not to be found.'

'And you?' Tizzie thought of her ending to Finnigan's story. 'Didn't you ever come back?'

'Oh, I *thought* about coming back,' Mum said, 'and once I nearly did, when you were a baby, Tizz. I got a train all the way to Gloucester, and then I lost my nerve. I just wandered round the shops and then went back to London. I was scared of what I might find here.'

'Scared!' Tizzie had never thought Mum was afraid of anything.

Mum nodded. 'I don't mean scared of you,' she told Finnigan. 'Scared of unearthing so many secrets, I suppose. Scared of becoming Greta again, when I'd almost forgotten what Greta was like. So I ran away again.'

'And you took to cooking?' Finnigan said.

'I did. I never settled at school, or cared much, and we were always moving. But cooking was something I could do. I was *hungry*! Always hungry. Ravenous. And I cooked, and cooked, and didn't need to eat much – it was the cooking I liked. Planning meals and making them. That's what I'm good at.'

'You certainly are,' Finnigan agreed. 'A marvel.'

Tizzie said, 'But you never stay in one place. Like Nannina. We're always up and off somewhere new.'

'I know.' Mum gave a sigh. 'I was always – always looking for something. Or running away from something. I don't know which.'

'So,' Tizzie asked, 'how did we get here?'

Mum smiled. 'I was looking through job adverts, when I saw this. Roven Mere, a big house near the village of Sleet. Roven Mere meant nothing to me – of course I knew this place as Paradise Hall – but I was curious to see Sleet again, so I applied, and got an interview. I was amazed to find that Roven Mere was my old home, and the man interviewing me was my own father. I couldn't look you in the eye,' she said to Finnigan. 'Said as few words as I could get away with. I couldn't believe it when you offered me the job!'

'I think,' said Finnigan gruffly, 'I *did* recognise

202

something of Greta. And it gave me pain. But some pain you just have to have. And now, now look!'

'But—' Tizzie was still confused. 'Why didn't you just go back to London? Why did you take the job?'

'I was more and more intrigued. Why was my father calling himself Finnigan, and talking about Lord Rupert as if he was someone else? He even mentioned Greta. So,' said Mum simply, 'I had to come and live here. I was fascinated.'

'Wasn't there anyone who knew you before?'

'Only Jack Doughty,' said Mum. 'He was here. But if I could fool my own father, I could fool Jack Doughty.'

'He told me he'd seen Greta!' Tizzie exclaimed. 'Did he mean – he saw *you*? Oh! Was it you who took the boat out, on the lake?'

'Yes.' Mum gave a secretive smile. 'It's my boat, after all! There are so many of my things here. I couldn't resist looking in my old room. This is my necklace!' She lifted the peacock-blue gemstone. 'You gave it to me,' she said to Finnigan, 'my birthday present, and I left it behind—'

'Your boat, your pony, your room, your everything,' said Tizzie. 'Oh, Mum, you had so much!'

'I know. Too much.'

'I wanted Greta for my *friend,*' Tizzie said, with a little laugh.

'Perhaps,' said Mum, 'she ought to be your friend. A better friend than she has been, at least.'

There was something – no, many things, so many –

Tizzie still didn't understand. She looked at Finnigan, who was smiling in a bemused sort of way, and asked him, 'But what I still don't get is – why did you – why did you pretend Greta was still twelve? That she was coming back any minute?'

He looked at her. 'Maybe I'm a bit too good at pretending. It was – a story I told myself. It was silly, and I knew it was, but all the same I couldn't stop believing it. I couldn't bear the truth, or what I thought was the truth – that I'd never see my Greta again. It's easier to live in stories, sometimes, when the truth is too hard to take. Only now,' he added, with a shake of his head, 'the truth is too *good* to believe. And who's to say that my believing in it didn't make it come true?'

Tizzie knew then that she loved Finnigan, for his doubt and his hope, for his hurt and his everlasting loyalty. Loved him more than she loved anyone else except – yes! – Mum. And it was all right, because Finnigan would, or maybe he already did, love her, too. Unless—

'Mum,' she said hesitantly. 'We're not going to move on again, are we? Are we, you know, staying?'

'Yes, Tizz. We're staying. This is our home.'

Tizzie took a deep breath, and looked around her – at the high hedges, the bees in the lavender, the dovecot waiting for its doves, and the house-roof rearing beyond. Home! Really home. She'd always felt that the house was waiting; what she hadn't realised was that it was waiting for *her*. Her and Mum.

'And—' It sounded a daft question, but she had to be sure. 'Am I still Tizzie?'

'Course!' said Mum, nudging her and making her sway. 'Who else would you be?'

'Most certainly you are!' said Finnigan. 'I don't know anyone more tizzieful. Anyone with more tizzieness about them. You're gloriously, tizzily Tizzie.'

25
Paradise Hall

At first it seemed that it would take lots of getting used to, and then it seemed that it had always been like this.

'Well! Well I never!' Mrs Crump kept saying. 'Why didn't you say?'

Will Crump: 'This is a turn up for the books!'

Jack Doughty: 'Greta back? I knew it all along. Knew she'd come.'

And Davy: 'What – you mean? – but how come – I don't get it. Duh?'

Finnigan only smiled. Smiled more than Tizzie had ever seen him smile before. He was a man who'd

206

lost all his happiness, but found it again.

'What now, though?' Tizzie asked Mum, back in Cloud Cottage that evening. 'What will we do? Will we move into the house, and be grand?'

Mum considered, brushing her hair in front of the bedroom mirror. 'No, I don't think we need do that. Why not just stay as we are? We can be happy here in the cottage, can't we?'

'But—'

'No buts. Let's just *be*. Things will sort themselves out.'

It wasn't that Tizzie didn't like Cloud Cottage, with her own room up in the eaves, and her view of the orchard. She loved it. It was just that, when she thought of the huge empty house, it seemed such a *waste*. All those rooms! All Greta's things!

Nannina was coming to visit on Sunday, catching the train from London. Mum was going to meet her at Gloucester station, and drive her here in the van.

Nannina. Angel – Angelina – Nina – Nannina. Tizzie had been forced to readjust her view of Nannina quite drastically. Abandoning Finnigan! Walking out and leaving him heartbroken! Because he had loved *not wisely but too well,* as he'd put it in the story. It couldn't be right, what she'd done.

'Don't go expecting miracles,' Mum warned. 'It's not a fairy-tale.'

Tizzie hadn't expected Nannina to bring the dogs with her, but as soon as the van pulled up and the door opened, they leapt out and started chasing each other round the courtyard: Benny and Bill, big, boisterous collies. And there was Nannina, climbing out of the passenger seat. Her hair was skewered into an untidy bun, her clothes were loose and flowing; she wore bright purple shoes with a daisy pattern on the toes.

'So! Here we all are, then.' She looked around her as if she'd been here only last week, instead of twenty years ago. 'Benny! Bill! Don't go getting into trouble.'

Tizzie couldn't imagine what would happen when Nannina and Finnigan met. Would they even speak to each other? At least, if they wouldn't, Roven Mere was a big enough place for each to stay out of the other's way. While she and Mum were showing Nannina round the garden – though of course Nannina had seen it all before, apart from the Knot Garden – they bumped into Finnigan coming up through the vegetable plots.

'Well, hello there,' from Nannina.

'Erm, yes. Good to see you,' from Finnigan. A formal shaking of hands, and an exchange of pointless remarks about the weather and the flowers. Luckily, before the conversation ran down completely, like weakening clockwork, Jack Doughty ambled up the path with a basket of strawberries, and his dog Mac. When Benny and Bill saw Mac, there was a great deal of snuffing and hackle-raising, and a skirmish that looked likely to turn into a full-scale fight. By the time the dogs were separated, and strawberries spilled in the grass had been picked up again and some of them tasted, the sticky moment had passed. From then on Nannina and Finnigan seemed to agree to treat each other as old but rather distant acquaintances.

There was no question, none at all, of Nannina wanting to come back, or even of Finnigan wanting her to. She was a Londoner; she made it plain that one day in the country was quite enough.

'So! What are your plans for this great barn of a place?' she asked Finnigan over lunch. 'You used to say you wanted the place full of children's voices. Well, why not?'

Finnigan looked startled. 'What?'

'You've got enough money. Why not do something with it? Open up the place. Bring children here – city kids. Give them a treat! They'll think they're in a different world. You've turned it into a museum, a dead old museum no one ever sees – what a waste!'

Nannina in full flow was hard to resist. By the time lunch was over, she'd outlined plans for holiday weeks, school groups, special weekends: courses in puppetry and painting, model-making and gardening, canoeing on the lake, pony-riding, walking and orienteering. Tizzie saw the place full of life and activity and excitement; herself and Davy showing the new arrivals around, having big noisy meals, going on outings, learning all sorts of new things.

'Yes. Yes, you're quite right,' Finnigan kept saying, in a daze. 'Absolutely right.'

'What about you, Mum?' Tizzie asked, as Mum had

made no comment. 'What do you think?'

'I want to cook,' Mum said.

'Well, you *do* cook.'

'I want lots of people to cook for. I want to run my own cafe. That's what I've always wanted. I'll call it Margareta's, maybe, or Greta's, or Morag's – I'm not sure yet. And when there are no children here, we'll open for other people, people from the village, and tourists and visitors. We'll do special Christmas meals, and Hallowe'en, and Divali and Chinese New Year. I'll need helpers. I'll need to take over the dining-room. I'll need to plan it—'

'Excellent!' Nannina clapped her hands. 'There we are. All settled.'

It was a game, playing, pretending, adding more and more details: but later that evening, when Nannina and the dogs had gone, Tizzie heard Mum and Finnigan talking over the ideas in the kitchen, quite seriously.

'Should we change the name back to Paradise Hall?' Mum was asking.

Finnigan considered.

'No. No. It's Roven Mere, now. And I'm still Finnigan. Lord Rupert feels like a different person.'

'But surely,' said Mum, 'you'll move out of the caravan? Have a nice room in the house?'

'Oh no, I don't think so. We're quite happy, me and Small,' said Finnigan. 'We've got everything we need. *More* than everything. We'll stay as we are.'

Tizzie was thinking about Nannina. Whatever the

210

rights and wrongs of the Paradise Hall years, Nannina had lied, hadn't she? And because of her, Mum had had to lie, too. They'd made Tizzie believe that her grandfather had died, years and years ago, and she might never have known differently. Although Nannina had looked exactly the same as usual, she had changed, in Tizzie's view, as much as anyone.

New Nannina, new Greta-Mum, new *grandfather*. There was such a lot to get used to.

26

The Island on the Mere

'When I lived here,' Mum said over breakfast, on the Saturday after Nannina's visit, 'I always wanted to have a picnic on the island.'

'And I promised you a rowing-boat,' said Finnigan. 'But before the boat arrived, you'd – you know—'

'Gone,' Mum finished.

'But now there *is* a boat. And here are we. And here's a sunny day,' said Finnigan. 'Let's do it.'

Mum made quiche and salad for everyone else's lunch, and she and Tizzie made up a picnic, finding a real old-fashioned picnic basket to put it in. At midday they went down to the boat-house, the three of them, Finnigan carrying the basket, Tizzie with a blanket to sit on in case the grass was still damp.

There, tethered, rocking gently on the water, was the little boat, *Nevermore*.

'I'll row us across,' said Mum, climbing in. 'You can have a go later, Tizz.'

They took their seats: Mum facing Tizzie and Finnigan, who sat together on the little cross-bench, with the picnic and blanket between them. Mum pushed off from the boathouse wall, and they were out on the open water. Tizzie watched her lean and pull in the rhythm of the rowing; the dip of oars into greenish water, then the scattering of diamond drops as they lifted. It reminded her of Finnigan's first story.

As they neared the island, Tizzie saw how small it was: just a mound of grass, three small trees that leaned over the water, and a gravelly beach. Mum pulled in, grounding the boat on the shingle, then tugged off her shoes and socks and climbed overboard into the shallows. She pulled the boat high enough for Tizzie and Finnigan to disembark on to dry land, and tied the rope to a low branch.

'It's just about big enough for a tent,' Tizzie said, looking around. 'If I had a tent. Maybe Davy and me and Robin could camp out one night! I've never done that.'

'On really warm nights in summer,' Finnigan told her, 'you can sleep out in the open. Not even bother with a tent. That's even better. Lie in your sleeping-bag and look up at the stars.'

They ate their picnic – ham and crusty bread, Mum's little mushroom patties, and strawberries; sparkling wine for Mum and Finnigan, grape juice for Tizzie – sitting together on the grass, looking across the water at Roven Mere. The house, which had looked so bleak and forbidding to Tizzie at first, now seemed to call to her. She belonged to it. It was home, or would come to be home, in a way nowhere in her life had been before.

When they'd finished eating, Mum let Tizzie have a turn with the oars, and row back to the boat-house. It was hard to keep a straight course, and quite tiring, but soon Tizzie had learned how to steer, and how to dip and lift the oars without splashing.

'It'll be easier next time,' said Finnigan.

Tizzie thought of all she had to look forward to. On Monday, after school, Robin was coming home for tea, and Davy was going to take them riding, on Ditty. Robin could ride a little, Tizzie not at all, but Davy said he'd teach them. Mum and Finnigan had even said that Kamila could come and stay, in the summer holidays. And then there were all the plans to be made. Finnigan had made appointments with his accountant and his bank manager; Mum was busy working out how to turn the dining-room into a café. They were hoping that the first groups of children would come next year, in the spring. Roven Mere would a busy, happy place, full of laughter and activity.

Tizzie watched Mum mooring the boat. She looked at the name, in yellow letters, and thought of its sad meaning: *never more, never more.* An idea came into her mind.

'Is there any of that blue paint left?' she asked Finnigan.

'Yes, in my workshop, I think. What do you want it for?'

Tizzie wouldn't say. She made them promise to wait; there was still some wine left in the bottle, so they didn't mind sitting in the sunshine for a bit longer, talking over their plans.

In the workshop she scurried about, finding the blue paint, a brush, and an old stick for stirring. Carrying them, she ran back, panting, puffing, hardly able to wait.

At the boathouse, she stirred the paint and dipped her brush. With Mum and Finnigan watching, she carefully painted out the letter 'N'.

Immediately, wearing its new name, the boat looked far jauntier; it seemed to sit more lightly in the water.

Finnigan laughed. 'Yes, of course. *EVERMORE!* How clever of you, Tizzie.'

'Because,' said Tizzie, 'we're going to live here for ever more. Together. Aren't we?'

'Yes,' said Mum. 'We are.'

Tizzie wished she'd looked for yellow paint as well. If she'd brought that, she could paint out the first E, and replace it with the flourishing Evershall E. It was hers, now! She was an Evershall, like Greta, like Mum. Tizzie Evershall.

She'd do it tomorrow.

Oddly, the Greta of her imaginings still seemed to be here: laughing in the background, hiding just out of sight. Like an invisible friend, an invisible sister.

She began to think that one day she might try to write a story. Stories were in her blood, after all: she knew that, now. She'd inherited them from Michael Rafferty, the father she would probably never know; and she'd inherited them from Finnigan, too. Her father and her grandfather.

Stories. They're everywhere, she thought. You never know where they start, and you certainly don't know where they'll end. If they ever *do* end.

Once there was a man who lost all his happiness, but found it again. That was Finnigan's story.

Mum? *Once there was a girl who had everything a girl could want, but who left it all behind . . .*

Nannina? Tizzie wasn't sure what Nannina's story was – only bits of it – so she wouldn't try to tell that one, not yet.

And me, she wondered? *Once there was a girl who expected nothing but bad, but found nothing but good . . .*

Yes, thought Tizzie. I like that for a start.